ADVANCE PRAIS

MW00782948

"The stories in *Sad Grownup* contemporary and timeless and engage American life today in ways that are at turns funny, insightful, and wise. I couldn't stop reading."

–Cara Blue Adams, author of *You Never Get It Back*

"Wise, inventive, and funny, *Sad Grownups* is also an incisive collective portrait of contemporary Americans: each story distinctly and decidedly itself, gathered together into a sometimes delightful, sometimes sobering snapshot of what it is to be alive today. In the tradition of Amy Hempel and Lorrie Moore, Amy Stuber is as sharp as she is tender, a delight to read."

–Kate Doyle, author of *I Meant It Once*

"These seventeen varied and remarkable stories often start with a curious premise, but open into complex, believable worlds, with rich characterization. Smart, funny, spooky and melancholy, *Sad Grownups* is full of unique gems that come together into a rewarding whole."

–Dan Chaon, author of *Stay Awake*

"Stories that hold the grief of the whole world but also the imaginative exultation of trying to live in it. Stuber writes sentences that are in a class of their own—flexible enough to twist from heartbreak into hilarity, full of observations so precise they leave you gasping. *Sad Grownups* is a brilliant collection."

–Clare Beams, author of
The Garden and *The Illness Lesson*

"If emotions had geographical locations, then Amy Stuber's deeply moving short story collection *Sad Grownups* took me to those places, but in no way was it like riding a Greyhound bus, hitting each city, each emotion, one at a time. Each story took me to the joyfully complex, lovingly hated yet adored world as it is today, and did so with some of the funniest and saddest characters I've read in quite some time. Reading these stories, I lost myself, and when I put the book down, I found myself anew. *Sad Grownups* is a remarkable debut story collection by a writer who I already want more from."

–Morgan Talty, national bestselling author of
Night of the Living Rez and *Fire Exit: A Novel*

"Amy Stuber's stories are about your neighbors and friends, the people you think you know, and what they are all hiding from you: the truth, which is that we are children and will remain so, that we are performing and we don't know it. Stuber's characters fumble through adulthood, they endure the confusing mysteries of growing up, they try to connect and instead create disasters. *Sad Grownups* marks the arrival of an erudite, controlled, and generous voice from the heart of America."

–Richard Mirabella, author of
Brother & Sister Enter the Forest

SAD GROWNUPS

Short Stories

Amy Stuber

STILL
HOUSE
PRESS

All inquiries may be directed to

Stillhouse Press
4400 University Drive, 3E4
Fairfax, VA 22030
www.stillhousepress.org

Stillhouse Press is an independent, student- and alumni-run nonprofit press based out of Northern Virginia and operated in collaboration with Watershed Lit: Center for Literary Engagement and Publishing Practice at George Mason University.

Library of Congress Control Number: 2024940299

ISBN-13: 978-0-9969816-6-8

Jacket Art and Design: Michael McDermott
Interior Design: Paul Logan IV

Previously Published Stories

"Day Hike," *The Common*, October 2024

"The Last Summer," *The Missouri Review,* Summer 2023

"Little Women" (originally published as "LittleWomen-House), *Northwest Review*, February 2022

"Ghosts," *Craft*, Fall 2022

"Doctor Visit," *Cincinnati Review*, Fall 2021

"Our Female Geniuses" (originally published as "How We Want Our Female Geniuses," *The Florida Review*, Fall 2021

"Dead Animals," *Joyland Magazine*, July 2021

"Dick Cheney Was Not My Father," *The Common*, June 2020

"Sad Grownups," *Witness*, Fall/Winter 2020

"More Fun in the New World," *Ninth Letter*, Fall 2019

"Corvids and Their Allies," *TriQuarterly*, July 2019

"Edward Abbey Walks into a Bar," *Joyland Magazine*, February 2019

"People's Parties," *Copper Nickel*, Fall 2018

"Wizards of the Coast," *Faultline*, June 2018

For Matt, Edie, and Ben

Contents

Day Hike

Alice wants to walk on the trail, but Renee wants to wander. At least, that's what I imagine.

Maybe Alice tells Renee, "It takes two hours to get to the lake. Let's keep moving." And probably Renee heads down offshoot paths to get closer to the falls. In the first half hour, on their way to the lake at the peak, they see a fox, a mother and baby moose, and three animatronic-looking deer.

"What if they aren't even real?" Renee says, pointing to the deer. She drinks too much from her water bottle too early while Alice conserves. "What if they are humans in deer suits?"

"Funny," Alice says, but she doesn't show teeth.

"Okay, I'll shut up," Renee says, and they stop where a Fiat-sized rock sits beside a green field with a river unfurling into it.

Alice climbs onto the rock and sits. The silver-backed leaves of the Aspen trees flutter. White blobs of fungi puff out of a crack in a nearby pine.

"I guess we're stopping," Renee says. She takes off her backpack and pulls out the trail mix she would never buy at home, nuts filmy with salt and cranberries covered in white sugary stuff the packaging claims is yogurt.

The trip was Alice's idea and involved three flights, two transfers, and a two-hour rental car ride from the airport that ended at a cabin with a door knocker made of an elk's foot. They spent the first two days doing short hikes to adjust to the altitude, as Alice said was recommended. A walk around a lake. A drive into the national park to see a historic trout camp. Some kayaking. Ice cream while watching kids dig in the sand by the water. A bookstore. Petting other people's dogs. Dinner at a lodge where the salmon was cooked so much Renee whispered it was "beyond dead and maybe reincarnated." It wasn't that funny, but Alice laughed, and this made Renee happy. They did the obligatory beginning-of-vacation fucking on the screened-in porch and were startled by a moose that wandered into the yard, looked up at them with big, blank eyes, and proceeded to decimate a shrub outside the porch screen. *This, this is really living*, Renee thought while above the moose's antlers, the stars and the clouds made a pattern against the nighttime sky.

A family passes on the trail near where Alice and Renee sit on the rock. Every person in the family wears some version of the American flag: shorts on the dad, a hat on the mom, the boy and girl, both looking sweaty and miserable, in matching flag-adorned t-shirts.

It's all so stock and on the nose that Renee almost laughs out loud. It's close to the Fourth of July, a holiday Renee and Alice both hate, especially Alice, for the forced nationalism and loud noises.

"Are we getting close?" the flag shorts dad says, looking at Alice. He wipes his brow with a bandana and laughs. "We're not the most experienced hikers." The man's backpack is one of those insubstantial ones they give away at a hospital or a car dealership. Renee sees him look at her breasts and look away.

Alice puts her phone down on the rock and says, "You mean to the meadow or the lake?"

"The lake," the woman says. She's unsmiling below aviator glasses and carrying those poles you hold out in front of you like antennae. The kids glare at each other. The girl sighs and rolls her eyes. The boy wears thick glasses and is panting. He kicks the ground and says something under his breath. *There's really no telling*, Alice thinks, *how your kids will turn out.*

Alice and Renee have spent the last few months in the trenches of a discussion about having or not having children. At forty, they're both aware of their shelf lives for biological children. Alice sometimes imagines herself in the park looking at birds with a small boy, but she also feels hemmed in by the idea of parenthood being a required hoop to jump through to give their lives meaning. Renee's own mother died young, at just thirty-nine when Renee was starting college. It makes Renee panicky about her lateness to the big things in life. Her ghost mother appears sometimes in front of Renee, in the kitchen, for example, beautiful in a silk robe, tapping an old Timex and mouthing, *tick-tock.*

"Oh, yeah, you're pretty close to the lake, not far at all," Renee says to the man. Alice pinches her thigh, but Renee doesn't react.

"Okay, then, we soldier on," the man says. "You two," he says and pauses, "have a good time." And the family continues up the path.

"Why the hell did you lie?" Alice whispers. "The lake is definitely more than an hour from here." She looks at the trail map she photographed on her phone.

"I don't know. I didn't have the heart to tell them," Renee says and grabs the trail mix. She tips the bag into her mouth and lets too many nuts and dried cranberries tumble in. The reality is she didn't like the family for how they looked at them and didn't mind the thought of them suffering slightly. She doesn't want to admit this to Alice, but she's pretty sure Alice already knows.

The sun comes out from behind a cloud like one from a children's book, and the rocks on the trail sparkle.

Alice points to a spot below the trail where a deer is lying in the grass making a mini crop circle.

"Is it dead?" Renee asks.

"Of course it's not dead. Not every prone thing is dead. It's sleeping."

This is how they are: Alice and Renee, together two years now.

(My friend Sela, *the writer*, drinks her drink and pulls at one of her three gold chains, each with a different charm: wishbone, letter S, pineapple. The bar where we always meet after work is uncrowded, and the music, something I recognize from my childhood but can't name, is loud.

She leans in, holds her paper straw in front of her, and says, "So, don't take this the wrong way, but I was wondering. Aren't Alice and Renee each a bit too much of a type? I wanted them to be maybe more nuanced. Also, I don't know if you *can* write about lesbians, like, if you're *allowed*. You're, what, loosely bisexual at best?"

I blink a few more times than necessary and look over at the window glass that reflects a series of electric cars, tiny and jewel colored, all plugged in and waiting to go somewhere else. Sela and I met in a creative writing class in college, taught by a famous writer who was more beautiful than should be acceptable for someone also so creative.

I reach out to adjust her necklaces. "I'm more than loosely bisexual," I say to her, but my cheeks go red.

Between the two of us, Sela is the more successful. She has a book deal. Better hair and clothes. A living mother who calls her the right number of times a week. A one-bedroom instead of a studio. I can try to make myself feel better by thinking all of this makes her uninterestingly typical, but the truth is, I know she will probably always have an easier time than me, will always be happier than me, and it stings to think it.

Sela laugh-coughs and says, "Come on, girl, you know what I mean.")

Alice and Renee ascend a series of unshaded switchbacks without talking while birds they can't see make noises in the trees.

The thing about even thinking about having children is that it calls to mind your own mother and yourself as a child, both things that can be fraught, as if strung together by a series of trip wires. *Remember how you decapitated Barbies,* Renee's ghost mom says. She's smoking a thin cigarette and listening to Elton John. *Remember the kitten you couldn't handle,* she says, and she exhales smoke that blurs her face.

"Did you hear something?" Renee asks. She's convinced they will see a bear, even though a ranger at the start of the path by the trail sign told them it was "highly unlikely."

"I did not," Alice says.

"It's not supposed to storm, is it?" Renee asks Alice, who is looking down at her phone. The clouds coming over the ridge above them are more gray than white, and the wind heaves in the trees.

"I'm not getting service here, but I checked a while ago, and there was nothing on the radar."

They cross over two logs that make a bridge. Renee feels like she's Laura Ingalls Wilder and longs for a time before cars, before sea levels rising. Alice wonders about the process of cutting the logs to make a bridge: as in, did it occur somewhere else, and the logs were hauled here, or did someone bring the saw on site?

Alice and Renee are both still relatively new to being with women, so there is that breath of awkwardness before they even use the word lesbian. It sounds antiquated too, but queer doesn't feel like theirs to say. They were both married to men when they met, and soon after meeting, they left their husbands. Renee moved into Alice's apartment, a place nicer than anywhere Renee lived before, a place that contains things she's never owned before, like a ceramic dish for roasting garlic or a mesh bag to put bras in, so the dryer doesn't mangle them.

When they first got together, they decided their marriages were flawed because they were with the wrong people (men) and that being together after that would somehow lead to a better life. It hasn't worked that way. Renee is still often impulsive and temperamental, and Alice is still sometimes icy and imperious. Also, the easy way they left their past relationships sits like a block between them. They have happy stretches, though. Sometimes they watch a whole season of a bad reality show in one weekend while sharing pea protein ice cream and rubbing each other's feet.

Alice stops to photograph a cluster of meaty, speckled mushrooms.

"Ooh, maybe we should forage," Renee says.

"These are incredibly poisonous," Alice says.

"Oh, okay then," Renee says and walks faster, ahead of Alice on the trail.

"Are you still mad?" Alice asks, even though she knows she should leave it alone. Last night, after the moose, Alice told Renee she didn't know if she had it in her, a baby—kids in general.

Renee then went into the second bedroom without saying anything. When Alice tried to lie down by her, Renee asked her to leave. The temperature in the mountains was higher than normal, but neither of them felt okay about turning on the air conditioning. Renee, alone in the room, spread herself out on the bed and watched food reels on Instagram until she was able to fall asleep with one leg hanging off the mattress and one arm above her head and the fan on high. She dreamed of pudding made of bananas and protein powder and woke up feeling terrible.

"Are you saying I shouldn't be mad?" Renee stops and reties her shoes. A bee hovers over an orange flower before disappearing inside of it. In a few days, they will be back at desk jobs in their respective tall buildings, sending emails, taking elevators down to lobbies, and trying to decide what carryout sounds best.

"That's not what I'm saying at all. Look, I'm sorry," Alice says, and from behind, catches one of Renee's hands, and Renee lets her hang onto it so they are connected for a few strides until Renee shakes her hand free. It's enough for Renee to feel warm, though, to feel less alone. Her ghost mom says, *You've always been so needy, Renee*, because this was a lesson Renee's mom gave her: to be tough and unyielding was preferable to being ready to receive love, and though Alice is good at making her exterior rock-like, Renee is not. Renee wants to yell back to her ghost mom: *It's true! It's true.* She is soft, and though she once thought that at forty she might have grown out of the things that make her feel porous and child-like, she has not.

(On the way from drinks to the second bar with a bocci court on the back patio where we are supposed to meet up with two men from Sela's work, Sela says, "I didn't want you to feel weird about the book thing, so I didn't mention it initially. I just—I know you've been trying to get an agent for-fucking-ever. It's honestly a racket anyway, the black hole that opens up the second you send something off to them, it's like, *hello? Did you not tell me you wanted this?*"

One of Sela's heels gets stuck in a street grate in front of the bar, and I think, *This is why block heels are better for the city, Sela,* but she gets it loose with a small tug. Behind the tinted glass, I can see the outlines of people but not their faces. I reapply my lip gloss, about which my mother might have said, "Orange is not a color meant for the lips."

Sela leans closer to the glass to see herself better, pulls the gloss from my hand, and uses it, too. "Anyway," she says as she's dabbing at her mouth with her pinky, "this place is hilarious. Bocci? Really? I feel like it should maybe be, like, shuffleboard, something old school but not with a veneer over it, you know?"

"Yes, for sure, shuffleboard would be better," I say and put the lip gloss back in my bag. I've been in the city for three years post-college, and Sela—though I don't always like her—is my best friend.

Being an adult in the world is a wilderness, though, and one is allowed to do all the things that the strictures of childhood did not allow, even though sometimes its boundlessness can feel confining. All that space. All that thought about who you are supposed to be and aren't yet and maybe won't be anyway.

In the bar, Sela sits next to the cuter of the two men and grabs his hand immediately, and it's clear right then that she will fuck him later, and I will go home to watch a show about people working on rich people's boats, and I'll have a quick thought, like an insect alighting on a hand before flying somewhere else, about calling my mother and realize for the thousandth time that she's dead.)

A plane goes by overhead, one of those military ones that's louder than a commercial jet. Renee puts her hands over her ears.

"Woo-hoo!" someone yells from ahead of them on the path. The American flag family is coming back toward them. Their faces are red, and they look defeated and sweaty. Renee and Alice step to the side so the family can pass.

"There was no lake," the dad says. "At least not one we could find." He's trying to be friendly, but he's also gritting his teeth. Flag mom says nothing and stabs her poles ahead of her in the dirt and keeps walking. The two kids stare down at the path and try to keep up with her.

The dad sighs in a dramatic way, says, "Oh well." He lingers. His family keeps walking, and in a minute, they are out of sight.

"Did you lie about the lake?" the man says. His face is as ruddy as cowhide.

Renee starts to say something about the lake, an apology maybe, an equivocation, but Alice looks at her like *don't*, so she says nothing. Renee's ghost mom is there. She calls the man a *piece of work*. She says he's *up to no good*.

The man shifts his feet and puts his hands on his hips. "You can tell me, really. I won't be mad," he says to Alice and Renee. He walks closer until he's a few inches from them where they are backed up by a stand of trees and shoulder to shoulder.

They are at a juncture above a big meadow where the path curves along the side of the mountain. On the right, Aspens make a barrier wall, and on the left, the mountain drops off. Buttercups and sage grow out of the rocks near the edge. The meadow far below radiates an almost fluo-rescent green.

As a child, Alice organized her toys as if they were in a card catalog: alphabetically. Blocks to the left of dolls and animals (stuffed) to the left of blocks. When Renee was a child, she was into motocross and pulled crawdads from a creek with her mother who boiled them in a copper pot.

There's no sound but the wind. "Really, I won't be mad, it'll be like we're in on a joke. You know, ha ha," He reaches one red hand toward Renee, who is a few inches closer to him.

It's then he loses his footing. Or maybe it's then Renee taps him with her forefinger, or maybe she exhales in a way that somehow carries force, or maybe she pushes him with her whole hand. Later, they won't remember exactly what happened. Their brains will have reknitted the series of moments together. When Renee can't sleep that first night back in the city, when someone is yelling on the street, her ghost mom is there by the window in her robe, her hair loose on her shoulders, shaking her head saying, *Oh, you know.*

To Renee, the sound of him falling is like the sound of a full bag going down the long, dark trash chute in their building. To Alice, the sound of him falling is like the subway train at a distance rumbling closer. This is the thing: there is a space that will always be between them. A cloud, an exhale, a sigh, a gasp.

(Sela, drunk, leans in and scream whispers, "Don't you love that we're eating nachos like we're straight out of the 1980s, like fucking keto or whatever doesn't even exist, like bodies don't exist, like we're just nacho-eating blobs bobbing through life without any worries?" Sela's phone buzzes. She picks it up and puts it down. "God, my fucking mom again," Sela says. "I can't take another video of like, a chicken and a goat who are best friends."

I wouldn't mind seeing the chicken and goat friends video. In fact, I'd watched a whole series about unlikely animal friends and had, over those weeks, grown sure that sometimes crows on power lines were talking directly to me.

The two men from Sela's work drink sour beer and play pool. I push my drink too hard, and it tumbles onto its side. The ice and liquid roll a small lake over the table. Some of it drips onto Sela's lap before she can jump away, so she's sticky with whiskey lemonade, and I let it sit there for what feels like a full minute without jumping up and doing that nice friend thing of trying to dab it away.

"It's fine, it's fine," she says one too many times and then settles back onto her stool. "Okay, so I was thinking about your story," she starts up again, "and maybe there should be more of like a motivating factor for the motherhood thing for Renee, like why now?" Sela shakes her hair out of a clip and sets the clip on the table. She says, "All I'm saying is it would help the story's emotional resonance to know *why kids, why now.*"

She gets up to go to the bathroom and leaves her phone on the table. I pick it up. It's not password protected. I open her texts and heart all five of the most recent ones from her mom and then type: *lol mom ur the best,* and it gets hearted by Sela's somewhere-out-there mom immediately. Sela takes forever in the bathroom, so there's enough time for me to imagine saying to her, to even sit at the table and make my mouth run through the words: *I don't know, Sela, sometimes people just do things.*)

Alice goes to look over the edge first, and Renee can tell by the way Alice's shoulders untense that the man is not dead.

"Help me, you cunts," the man yells, and it's exactly what they expected him to yell, but very soon after, he says, "Just help me."

Beyond the ledge is a drop and then another ledge and then a more extreme drop. The meadow grass below where he's lying on the outcropping bends with the wind.

They could leave him. Eventually, he might make his way up to the path, or his family will reel back their steps and shout for him, or someone else passing will hear him. Or maybe—and this is unlikely—he will fall more, drop down to the meadow below, and mountain birds will pick apart his body.

Renee moves past Alice and climbs down to the man, and Alice holds onto Renee's arm to keep her steady.

"I can get back up myself," he half grunts, but he can't. His face and leg are bleeding into the dirt. His string back-pack is all the way down the side of the rock wall like a sad dead bunny on the floor of the meadow. Whatever was in it is lost.

In a chain of three people, they inch him over the few feet he's fallen until they are all back on the path. When they see he can stand, when it seems clear nothing obvious is broken, when he spits on his hands and wipes them, dirty and wet across the blood on his face, Alice and Renee take off running, alongside the path above the meadow and then back through the trees and all the way to the lake. It's just as pretty as the guidebook said it would be. Pines rise up on all sides. Wildflowers skim the edges. Soaked logs lodge at its perimeter.

"Oh my fucking god," Renee says, and Alice says back, "Oh my fucking god." They lean hands onto thighs and breathe heavily. Renee even starts laughing. She stops at a spot that's flat and green and right by the water.

"Are we not going to talk about what happened?" Renee says.

"Let's not," Alice says. She wipes her face with her shirt sleeve.

"Okay." She pauses and counts to ten. "Really? Not at all?"

Alice doesn't answer. Her breath starts to even out. She does a series of slow inhales and exhales.

"We should live here," Renee says to break the long silence. "Why is our whole life about labor? Maybe if we lived here, it could be about something else, something better." Renee lays completely flat on her back, spreads her arms out, and closes her eyes. *America*, she thinks, *is dumb and exhausting, gone in all the wrong directions.*

"I don't know. I like our life," Alice says. She knows what Renee means, though. Still, it's a luxury to want to carve a utopia and pocket yourself away while the whole rest of the world unravels. "You're going to get a million bug bites," Alice says.

"I don't care," Renee says.

Alice lies back next to Renee, and their arms touch all the way down, shoulder to wrist. Whatever complexity had been making a taut wall between them dissolves.

How were we ever not together, is something Renee almost says to Alice but doesn't. *This could last*, is something Alice thinks but will never speak.

"Okay," Alice says after many minutes without noise. "We should go."

They stand and start making their way down, down, down.

The sky is blue over the peak. This is how the weather is here: one thing one minute and another the next. They keep looking for but not seeing more animals. They both worry about the man but don't mention it. They are slow around all the turns, though, thinking he might be waiting.

After this, they will hike back to their car, sleep, wake, pack, get on a plane, eat circular pretzels, drink vodka tonics, Uber back to their apartment, light candles that smell like flowers and spices, eat wood-fired pizza, and try to sleep seven hours before going to work in the morning. Still, it's something for them to be here, now, with trees buzzing, flowers trembling, sky blue, their hands alive from the adventure of all of it. The lake, now far behind them, still holds its picture of the sky. They stop and get out their last snack, an expensive chocolate bar they pass back and forth.

"I hope there won't be cops waiting for us at the bottom or something crazy," Renee says.

"No," Alice says. "This is a story that man won't tell anyone."

"When we get home and tell our friends about this, they won't believe us," Renee says.

"It's like something out of Flannery O'Connor," Alice says.

"Except no one is murdered," Renee says.

"Yet," Alice says, and they both laugh. Renee's two front teeth are smeared with chocolate. Alice stops on the trail, pushes Renee against a tree and kisses the chocolate off Renee's teeth, licks, sucks, sticks her hand into Renee's pants, and for once doesn't wonder if anyone is around.

"Maybe we could," Alice says, and Renee knows she means: *baby*.

Renee's ghost mother is there. She doesn't laugh. She cackles. *You, with a baby*, she says. Her breath is a cavern inside of which Renee can see her whole childhood. *Look at you*, her mother says then, *living your best life*. It's not nice, though. It's a knife.

(The next morning at brunch, Sela looks like she has smudged her eyeliner to appear glamorously world weary. She leans forward so her tits hang just right. She says, "Hey, girlie, I'm sorry. Your story was actually really good. You had me thinking they were going to get, like, eaten by bears or fucking assaulted. But, like, I wonder if the flag bro should actually die? And for it to be this super dark moment, like he could die in a really weird, troubling way? Like a wind gust comes, and the man is impaled by a tree branch or something, like something you'd never expect?"

The thing is: there are only a few stories. Someone meets someone. Something unusual happens. Someone dies. People are sad, and they try to be happy. Adults carry their sad baby selves around with them their whole lives and are sometimes stern with them and sometimes sweet. Together, they hit against things, and maybe they come out better, or maybe they come out the same.

Servers tool around the room with croissants on pink, pearly plates and iced matchas with their bamboo straws rattling glasses. The day outside the window is sunny, and it's nice that it's a Saturday, and there's nothing else I have to do. I stand and regret the lace-edged white socks Sela talked me into buying to wear with my loafers. I pull cash from my bag, think of my mother's face wide and open, when we were in those long waiting months, when life felt like a short sentence with a visible period. I set the cash on the table, and say to Sela, "Death doesn't have to be a spectacle. Sometimes it just happens," and walk into the late morning where dog walkers pull along packs of dogs, and people sit alone but happy-seeming on benches. It's one of those movie moments: the light is right on the trees and buildings, so right that if I took a selfie, I might, for once, actually like it. I decide to become someone who owns kitten heels and oversized blazers, someone who walks with purpose, someone who leaves behind naivete with intention. Maybe my life will be the better one.)

The plane goes by again, coming back from wherever it was, this time lower and louder. *America, America,* the plane seems to be saying, brash, pulsing, and generally too much. It doesn't matter that Alice and Renee almost never drive, that they eat organic, that they use rechargeable batteries, that they set their AC to 76 except on the hottest days. The world, well, the people of the world, may still end before the child they have—the children they have, two of them— grow old. No amount of worry and planning can change that.

A deer walks behind where they are standing, and they are too busy to see it. Its fur is matted in spots, maybe from a tangle of barbed wire or a winterlong skin ailment. The deer watches them from behind the tree: blink, step, blink. The world right then is circles in circles in circles, and time is a stupid bee buzz you don't ever want to hear again. *Make it good, make it mean something, make it matter,* Renee's ghost mom says.

Anyway, tomorrow they will be home.

Little Women

Little Women House: Victoriana of the dunes. Sepia is the word that comes to mind. Unvarnished wood in the way of a commercial for antiquity. The sky is orange on the horizon. Fires glow through the windows. From the right angle, the window glass looks coated in butter. Someone managed to coax a flowering vine around a trellis. Cloying, yes. Maybe not real. Fake or real, no one cares.

The House Manager holds auditions to fill each role: Amy, Jo, Meg, Beth. The Amys flounce and have demands. A few of them sit for thirty minutes in an idling Escalade, and the shadows of their elbows and hands as they apply gloss and setting spray look like swooping crows. The Jos are full of proclamations. They carry cross-body bags and read political treatises or thin volumes of old poetry while leaning in the shade of the eaves. It is easy to separate the Megs. They make lists in the Notes app on their phones and wear hats to protect their skin from the sun, which isn't closer but feels closer—hotter at least. A handful of sad Beths stand in line by the portable toilets. They are all getting their periods at the same time, and they find Diva cups *so* complicated, something they say to anyone who will listen.

Beyond Little Women House, a hive of Houses pockmarks the desert. The houses seem to hover on patches of grass that shouldn't grow on sand but are kept alive by trucked-in water. Inside the Houses, teenagers film themselves, and other teenagers in Boise or Lemont or Sacramento sit in bedrooms or stairwells or on buses and watch their phones as House teenagers brush teeth, text boyfriends, flop back on beds with friends, do rehearsed dances.

It is the end of everything (species, previously infallible trees, ease, acceptable sea levels, edible fish, computers as human-dominated plastic boxes), but no one wants to admit it matters. Scientists use giant cranes to drop ice blocks heavy as a hundred wooly mammoths into the cold waters at the poles to lower the water temperature by a few degrees, to give everyone this moment of, *okay, maybe we're not doomed,* but it doesn't last for long. So, they pretend; what are their options?

The House Manager at Little Women House tires of the day-long auditions. She smokes at the place where the sprinklered grass meets the sand, where a lizard glares at her from a rock. "This has gone on long enough," she says to the lizard, and she settles on one of each: one pretty Amy, one industrious and independent Jo, one practical Meg, one sad and always-dying Beth.

Amy sits in front of a mirror in a dressing gown meant for another century. She works it, though. She makes it look hot. She insists on being filmed in the most obvious poses. Even though it's un-nineteenth century, she does her nails in a gradient in various blues. She leans out open windows during golden hour, so her corset catches her breasts up higher, and there's that loose shake and flutter of flesh that makes you want to watch and then watch again.

On a Friday, Amy sits by the pool. The Meg flanks her. They both put their feet in the water. Like most outdoor water, it's no longer cold. Meg is tolerable to Amy, but mainly because she is useful. Amy can say, "Pass me the sunscreen," and Meg passes the sunscreen, even though it's almost empty. Amy assumes Meg will feel virtuous for having sacrificed her own skin to the desert.

Even though Amy's role is to look pretty, to be delicate and picture-like but then sometimes acceptably tempestuous, even though followers might describe her as "feminine," which somehow is a thing that still exists, though gender has been laudably chipped away, still, she is more of a boy in her head.

Before Little Women House, she worked in a restaurant, and she felt most at home and alive in the dirty basement of the restaurant smoking on an old couch with the cooks, all men, who talked about cars and cunts and all the hard-edged things that made her feel rough herself and with nothing small or pliant about her.

At night, The House Manager brings a vanload of men for Content. They film on the front porch, which The House Manager calls *the veranda*. They film in the living room, which The House Manager calls *the parlor*.

Amy sits on the plum-colored velvet couch. Many of the men, whom The House Manager will insist on referring to as *gentlemen callers*, bring her drinks. It's boring but not the worst way to move through a night, which The House Manager calls *the evening*.

One of the men sits next to her, talks about the weather, and then puts his hand under her skirt. It's a challenge because the skirt is what The House Manager might call *voluminous*.

Amy lets her mind wander. She's in the restaurant basement, and someone is grabbing her by the walk-in. Or she's out of the Little Women House corset on a Friday. She's rolling in the sand beyond the circle of the motion light, fucking, and you can't call it anything else. It's the height of life, really, for an Amy, to be urge and movement only. She's out of body. Or she's so much her body that's all she is.

Jo at the writing desk. Jo in a replica nineteenth century military jacket. Jo on a Friday, striding, which is hard to do in sand, but if anyone can do it, Jo can. Her brass buttons catch the light, which is glinty and relentless.

When she gets back to The House from her walk, early evening, before the men, her boots are full of sand she dumps in the fire. She looks at the flame and wonders at not feeling more special than she does. She carries a candle powered by batteries up the stairs to her room where she unrolls parchment and furrows her brow, thinking, as Jos do, about a lifetime of Impossible Choices. She writes a few lines about bleakness and wanting until the night sky is dark fur with punches of stars in clusters that scream out: there are Other Places, very far away.

TBH, the Jo story is a harder story to tell in the twenty-first century when they are all supposed to be all the things: pretty, productive, artistic, assertive, funny, submissive, in charge, living, dying.

Before the Friday van comes, The House Manager enters Jo's room without knocking and puts out a cigarette on the stone slab where Jo's fountain pen sits. She holds her phone in front of Jo's face and shows her a picture of a pretty girl who posts palm-sized poems about the leaves or wind.

The House Manager says, "Can't you post something like this? A short poem? Something nice?"

It angers Jo that there is almost no effort in it, that it is so soft and easy, but then her whole life is a defensive posture. It's part of why she came to Little Women House in the first place. A string of nothings in a middle state where she did gig work and rode a vintage bike through cemeteries on the weekends and tried not to think about the future. There, her fingers twitched when she walked from place to place, and the smallest things made her sad: a woman carrying a plastic-wrapped tray of sandwiches cut triangle-shaped into a church building or a man holding a sign trying to lure people into a new business that sold tea in bulk bins. All the human striving up against so much world dying, human dying. Sometimes, she made herself a ball in the cemetery and felt the name ghosts, the once-weres, descending on her and wanted, also, to be gone.

When the van rolls up to The House, Jo stays in her room and lets Beth talk her into henna tattoos of vintage type-writers up and down her forearms.

Later, when the van goes, Jo, still alone, lonely, sits on her bed and looks out the circular window and beholds scorpions flashing tails at each other on the patio and the crook of the moon over the desert, all of it like a stock image on a website, all of it more endless and boundless than she.

Meg spends Friday doing what now might be called crafting but in eighteen-something would have had no special label. She does cross stitch. She quilts. She churns fucking butter, and who knows where The House Manager got the cow-fresh milk and the churn, but The House Manager can work miracles. Within an hour, the video of Meg churning with the top buttons of her lace-edged floral dress unbuttoned while sweat gathers at the place where her chest meets her neck becomes one of the most-oft-viewed videos.

The House Manager says to Meg, "You're the sleeper, the underdog, look at you go."

A Meg isn't supposed to care because a Meg is a Meg, pretty enough but kind of background. But there she is, the unexpected star of the butter churn.

She'd spent high school strategically not eating until her arms and legs were tissue over twig. But all of that withholding, all those baby steps around the lunchroom and vomit splatter wiped away with brown paper in the communal bathroom, hadn't done anything for her, so she stopped. She went to college at a state school where there were hundreds of her. She worked the drive-through window at a coffee place and let the manager fuck her in the utility closet because she didn't think she deserved to say no. She ate everything: the chilled donuts and cinnamon rolls on trays in the walk-in. She pooled excess, let flesh make rings around her.

Now Meg waits in the living room on a Friday, that time between day and night. The House Manager sits next to her and eats mango out of a plastic container. She tells Meg, "Jesus, look at you, the translucence, the fucking tendrils, the goddamned milkmaid tits. You're it."

When they show up, the men circle Amy at first. Meg waits by the fireplace, and after thirty minutes, an hour, they come to her. It's too easy to get them to want her, and it's probably not even what she wants. For so many years, she worked to pull herself in at the boundaries so she wouldn't press against clothing or spread on bus benches or brush against other people. But people had still come for her body—men had—and as much as she hated it, hating it wasn't protection.

Beth is always dying. She is dying in The House, on the sand dunes, by the pool, in the grass that spreads fifty feet out from The House. She is dying in September and then October. She is dying near rattlesnakes that hide beyond the grass line, and maybe they could kill her more goddamned quickly, so she wills them forward, toward her, close, but then: nothing.

Before The House, she played bad piano songs at a restaurant that was the kind of place people chose for Valentine's Day. Everyone there was either in love or unexpectedly breaking up in dramatic ways, and she was in the background. She would play, and people would lean over tabletops to kiss. Even though Beth wasn't one of the kissing people, her throat would turn pink from the collarbone to the chin. A fucking hurricane could come, though, and the rain would turn the restaurant windows as opaque as inside a car wash, and still they would keep on, the declarations, the single red roses, the soft boxes stuffed with jewels.

Before the men come in the van on Friday, The House Manager leads Beth over to the piano in the room with the fireplace, sits her on a stool, and says, "Play something quiet and easy on the ears," and Beth does. It's evening all goddamned afternoon.

Sure, she is a good person, and that is something almost anyone can do if they try, so it feels lightweight, but still.

They keep on eating, sleeping, recording, as if one of them will not take ill on a random Thursday. (It will be Beth, everyone knows.) She would prefer dying on a beach to dying in bed, but almost no one gets to say. The sky around The House does its pretty sky things almost every morning and evening, so she films herself in front of the sky or at the piano, and the comments are things like "gorg" and "cutieee" and "ily bethie." It hurts to be her, but that's something she'll never say because of the vanity of it, the overwhelming silliness of it, when so many people are suffering before death and, for her, death will be the main suffering. But there are people in any group who carry some collective pain for the others, and she is that person and always will be.

She smiles while she sits at the piano, her hands fast spiders, before the men come in the van, while the sun is still up, and she can look shiny and full of wonder, and the others say, "Look at Beth, Beth is so good, Beth is the very best of us," and she hates them, but she can't help herself; she loves them, too.

Friday night is Content, so they perform. The House Manager eats and smokes and eats and makes demands: lean, soften, lounge, not like that, like this. This is what it means to be a woman in this world. Put a lot of justs in your sentences when talking to boys, to men, even if your idea is better; you don't want to look shrill or undermining. Say I'm sorry. Say it again while you're looking down and then laughing but under your breath because not too loud, ever. Check your DMs. Look pretty. Not too pretty. Everything is going away, but don't worry. A small waterfall near the pool forever recycles the same few gallons of water. Work out in the windowless room with the ellipticals. Don't worry. Meditate by a window with a single candle lit so you look like a person who knows how to be peaceful. Have women friends. But also, people should want to fuck you. But not the ones with girlfriends whose girlfriends you know and maybe have coffee with and run with because you are supposed to run, right? Run in those tights with patterns on them because your ass should look fuckable but not so much so that a stranger would slap it while you are minding your own business on a busy street or in a living room where the fireplace is always on, but hey, if you put your ass out there like that maybe people won't be able to resist it, and you should be okay with that because isn't being fuckable a goal? Walk to the edge of the grass that rings The House. Don't think about the end of the world. The man van leaves at two A.M., and The House Manager disappears. Then it's Little Women in the hot tub. Tilt the champagne flute. Act drunk even if it's ginger ale. Laugh in a way that brings to mind a bell. Let your toes drift up to the waterline so your pedicure shows. Sit until you're pruned and dizzy, until desert birds, fucking insistent sometimes, divebomb you in the chlorine water. Climb out. Enrobe. Hold hands with your housemates and walk beyond the grass circle out into the desert in starched cotton Victorian nightgowns because isn't that a vibe? Saturday now, early, so it's dark and where are the stars, are there stars, is it two A.M. or four A.M.? *Time,* Jo might say, *is a construct.* Beth is wan. Beth is hallowed. Beth is disintegrating. *Aren't we all,* Meg might say, the practical one, the one to take two truths and hit you over the head with them because she really can't help herself. There in the desert moonlight is the globular outline of Meg tits unmoored under cotton. Meg feels the tick tock of them and hates it. The body the body the body, something and then nothing. Everything, something and then nothing or something and then something else. Amy is beyond lip gloss for a moment. She's feeling the sand beneath bare feet, which was a stupid way to go out into the night desert. *My feet are getting scraped to shit,* Amy might say to sound tougher than she really is. *It would be so funny,* Amy wants to say, *for you to be able to see what your body becomes post-death.* For example, for the soul head of Amy to look on as the body decays, as the matter that was once Amy matter transmutes over time into other matter, a duck or a goddamned trailing vine hanging off a stupid decaying wooden house when humans are long gone, and maybe trees had memory this whole time and we refused to see it, so maybe only the trees remember humans, trees in some place far from the desert, full of majesty, standing taller than before, leaning with more glorious abandon than before, flutter their leaves, shine in the morning light. They emanate tree thoughts to whatever resilient animals make houses in their branches or sleep on the dried grass in the shade they make. Tree thoughts that speak to whatever parts and pieces in the landscape were once human, name ghosts, Little Women soul heads that were once sorrow and pretense and stabs at joy and are now something else because humans did themselves in, and the trees, no, they weren't kind old bark-sided gentlemen, they were always awaiting our departure, so much so that they look on at our once-human matter now non-human, now something better and think only: *humans, good fucking riddance.*

Dead Animals

Take me on a journey. Make me feel something. Surprise me. Make me change. Okay. *Okay.*

A dead cat sits near a trash can in an alley in The Mission. Step away. Scream if you're that kind of person. Stop. Wonder: did it eat poison? Did it, in some strange and unexpected manner, get electrocuted?

Backtrack.

Same alley, walking from point A to point B, Frida, thirty-four, sixteen towns in fifteen years. Retail worker, serial bad girlfriend, three green stars tattooed on her wrist that tell you she wanted to be someone who had tattoos but couldn't fully commit to something grand and meaningful, e.g., an old-timey ship on her upper back, going nowhere or, rather, going wherever she goes.

Tell me time and place.

June 2019. Frida works at a bookstore on Valencia where two women come every Saturday to ask her things like, "We don't want book club books, Reese Witherspoon shit, give us something better, Frida, save us," and she always does. Sabrina Orah Mark. "Oh, what she does with a paragraph, the beautiful economy! How she tells it like it is!" the women say. Mieko Kawakami, "Oh my GOD. So precise and simple. So much there about being a goddamned woman, Frida, what's next?"

So maybe it wasn't odd for them, after all the Saturday conversations, to ask Frida if she wanted to help with their daughter, Kyle. "She's thirteen, and she doesn't really *need* someone, but we don't want to leave her alone all day, and what's the alternative? She hates all the classes and camps. She's so cynical."

"Thirteen and cynical," the other mom said. "Imagine."

"Well, I was thirteen and drinking peppermint Schnapps from the bottle on ski lifts while giving grown-men ski instructors hand jobs for cash," the other mom said.

Frida, behind the barrier of the counter, watched as a man pulled books out and slid them back into the history shelf, war after war, not really looking at the book covers but instead making eye contact with Frida the whole time. Maybe she knew him. He looked familiar. His chin was sharp in a way that made her think of Ichabod Crane, but he was attractive enough and around her age. Still, she couldn't imagine fucking him, an actual three-dimensional man. All her recent interactions with men had been online, and it had soured her more than she wanted to admit to real life and real people.

Then first mom said, "We get it, you *did things*. You are very, *extremely interesting*. Frida gets it. Right, Frida?"

Frida looked away from bookshelf man, and when she looked back, he was gone.

Second mom joke-punched first mom on the shoulder, "Fuck off, I am interesting," but she was laughing and then asked, "What do you think? Will you take the job? We will pay you better than this." Her bangles clanked on her forearm, and she gestured out around the room where the books climbed above eye level with all their castigating spines.

Give me backstory. Let me hold this up next to something old to see why it matters.

Frida had decided early on that she would not really do relationships—monogamy—and she would not have children. It hadn't worked for her mother, for whom the motherhood part of her identity was always an afterthought. Exhibit A: by the time Frida was eleven, her mother had turned their garage into a shelter. This was generous and nice but also meant that, on any given morning, going to their one bathroom could mean an encounter with some man who'd crashed on the garage floor and to whom the back door was always open. Or Exhibit B: her mom kept maimed animals in crates in their mudroom, feeding them with droppers meant for baby medicine. Frida could remember walking into the mudroom at five A.M., unable to sleep, and there was the mother opossum her mom was rehabilitating in a dog crate with all the old blankets that had once been Frida's, her tail an obscenity, consuming her own sickly and apparently never-coming-back-from-it opossum baby.

Did she take the job anyway? Yes, she said yes.

The moms got her the following: a cloth wallet full of cash, their Uber on her phone, their Netflix and Hulu passwords, a key to the back door, the garage door opener. And then, for several days, Frida and Kyle did things that were inconsequential, really, but set the stage.

On a Monday morning, they went to Ocean Beach where the only person in sight was a man dressed like Mad Max of the sand dunes. Frida could hear the noise of other people, male voices somewhere in the dunes.

Even though it was cold, Kyle lounged on the sand and took pictures of a lurking V of pelicans and all their ghastly hovering. Kyle, Frida noticed, seemed to be someone who lounged without thinking of people watching her and critiquing her lounging. Kyle had long dyed-silver hair, played a green electric guitar, carried one and sometimes two vintage Russian cameras around her neck ("the Fed 3 is the best," Kyle told her), ate multiple packages of seaweed every day so her teeth were often flecked with dried green ("I don't give a shit about petty concerns with appearance").

Frida had done an experiment for the last few months where she eliminated mirrors from her house by covering them with photos of very old people. The idea was, instead of being bombarded by images of the young and the beautiful, to look right at the face of people who had lived through so many seemingly impassable things and were still going, who no longer had the luxury of façade, at least not in the same way. Sometimes, during this experiment phase and at night, when she wasn't corresponding with strangers online while intermittently staring out the window at the street below or making the zillionth bowl of pasta with butter like she was a toddler, she had embarrassingly basic philosophical thoughts, like, *What if getting through life and not stalling it or postponing it or pretending it wasn't happening was actually the goal? Or, in other words, what if getting old was the goal? Or would she ever figure out how to love and be loved the way people in movies seemed to do so easily, that delicate drop-off with a soft landing, as if it wasn't going to feel like two humans in giant robot suits, the clunk and crash of too-big limbs walking straight into a wall or off an unseen ledge?* That kind of thing. She fell asleep on these nights feeling childish and full of shame.

The next day, a Tuesday, Kyle and Frida ended up at a bar on Lincoln that served empanadas and a row of brash, light-up games along the back wall. Through the open door to the kitchen, a man used a saw that looked more home improvement than cooking to cut a whole leg off an animal that hung from the ceiling.

Frida and Kyle each got their fortunes from a machine by the bar where a plastic head told them about their future. Kyle was happy when the head told her she had unexpected fame and fortune coming. The head told Frida love was around the corner. The thing was, she did want to be loved, of course—who didn't—but for the most part, she felt like she had fallen asleep in one of those escape rooms where she knew she should work at her escape, but she was too inept to solve the series of puzzling mind games that would lead to her release, so she sat on a fainting couch instead and waited, for what she was not sure.

Frida had the bartender turn two of her last twenties into ones. She and Kyle played the basketball game endlessly, the one where the net kept moving farther away from you every thirty seconds while you tried to make shot after shot. She couldn't decide if that was like life, things slipping further and further out of your grasp, or if life was the opposite: things racing closer toward you in an imminent-car-crash way.

Regardless, Frida drank three margaritas before four P.M. and let Kyle have sips of each. A man at the bar whose face

she never saw paid for them, or so the server said each time
he brought one to her and set it at the small table next to
the basketball game.

Everyone has sub-basements. Everyone has things they
keep hidden: masturbating in the bathroom when everyone
else is downstairs watching a movie, not paying for the
toilet paper in the bottom of the Target cart, envying a
stranger's success. What is that thing about Frida? Tell
me that.

At night, in the room where she lived above the apartment that was ninety percent plants and one human
woman who greeted Frida in in the hallway in a different
language for each day of the week, Frida looked for men
online so she could talk to them about sex. If you met her,
she was a bit demure, or she was quietly matter of fact. She
gave off no clear and obvious sex vibe in person, but then
if you need sex to be a vixen, maybe that says something
about you.

Online, Frida was different, and her best night was when
five men in five different geographical locations, people
she only knew from a handful of selfies and the occasional
dick pic, would tell her how much and how they wanted
to fuck her or, mood depending, have her tell them how
much and how she wanted to fuck them. It was easier than
in-person dating, and it gave her the same satisfaction, the
same feeling of being desired and thus, maybe, desiring.
She also liked that these interactions ran their course, so
on any given night, she might be scripting some gymnastic
fucking with one man in Antigua while only early days
with a man in Seattle. At midnight or one A.M., she could
close her laptop and let the room go dark and again have

the relief of being a person who peed with her feet up on a stool in her terrible old pajamas while wondering if the water stain on the bathroom ceiling looked more like a chicken or a parrot, and this made her wonder why everything was a this or that, a comparison or duality, how on these nights, for example, she didn't know and then had to wonder if she was Frida or Frida, online or in-person, and then wonder if that even mattered.

In a story of consequence, you're riding in a car with people, and you think you're going to location X, you're excited about it, you're in a seat in the back on one of those long bench seats in an old car. You're looking outside. The windows are down. The wind in the trees marks the movement of things, time passing. But then even though the ocean is coming and going like it always does, even though the troupes of pelicans are rising and falling like they always do, even though you're expecting more of this kind of movement, its steadiness and the resulting pleasant lulling hum, the person next to you opens the door, and in an instant, you're rolling down the sand and rough grass that make the roadside. It hurts, but it's something and not at all what you thought it would be. Tell me that story.

The rest of the week went like this: a few hours in Kyle's apartment where her moms had left Post-its around the kitchen alerting them to food they should and should not consume. "Please don't eat the figs," but "there's fresh yogurt in the refrigerator." Kyle tore the Post-its off the counter and threw them in the recycling.

"They literally make their own yogurt," Kyle said.

In the moms' bedroom on Dearborn, Frida and Kyle ate all the yogurt from the glass container, their spoons clacking. They watched all the bad TV Kyle's moms asked her not to watch: *The Bachelorette*, home makeovers of various kinds, *The Kardashians* while Kyle stood on the bed and did her best Khloé Kardashian reenactment, "We all have to start somewhere," she said, her voice one part scratchy, one part baby. She flipped her hair and went on, "And doing something is better than doing nothing at all."

A truck went by too quickly outside with a bump and then a howling. She and Kyle ran out the front door and down the steps where an orange cat was flipping over itself, like its internal systems were shorting out. Frida didn't act quickly enough, but Kyle took off her jacket and wrapped up the cat who went suddenly leaden. A woman in a robe printed with thumb-sized tacos came out of her apartment screaming and took the cat bundle from Kyle and ran back into her apartment, and that was that. A dead cat was sad, but in the scheme of life's tragedies not the worst thing. Still, to have seen it losing its life like that, the dramatic hanging on that seemed to happen in the last moments, felt like something.

"I'm sorry you had to see that," Frida said to Kyle because it felt like something a parent would say, a mother.

"I'm okay," Kyle said, but she looked blown back and frazzled. Then one of the moms pulled into the driveway and opened the garage door.

"How was everything today?" the mom asked Kyle through the open car window, and Kyle changed her face completely and said, "Everything was really good!" and the two of them said goodbye to Frida.

When Frida walked the long way home later, after stopping to buy peanut butter and tampons and cookies made with

brown butter, around the block and down the alley, she saw
the cat on the ground by a trash can outside the woman's
back steps, the jacket cloth having fallen away, and the cat
rigid. The woman was nowhere to be seen. Frida arranged
the jacket around the cat so from a distance it might have
looked tucked in and sleeping. This was the thing, really,
the absolute craziness of life, that they were all supposed
to pretend the whole time that this end wasn't out there
on the horizon. She went back to her place and took a bath
with the lights off and one candle going on the windowsill.

    After the bath, one of the men Frida had been messag-
ing for several weeks, someone who claimed to work in IT
in Montreal, a man whose cock, if the one he'd sent her
several photos and even a short video of, was in fact his,
looked mottled and tilted but still generally okay, told her
he wanted to be waiting in her apartment when she came
home, hiding in a closet or the bathroom and surprise her,
fuck her with force while she's blindfolded, hands bound
and maybe he has a weapon, that's his fantasy. Frida knew
plenty of people were into this sort of thing, so no judg-
ment, but she wasn't one of them. "Maybe I already know
where you live," he typed and followed it with a winky
smiley face, even though they had both agreed previously that emojis were tiresome and over. In the week leading up to that Wednesday, they had talked in a jokey way
mainly about kicking, biting, pressing, and throwing, and
Frida had found that pleasing because she liked to think
of her Internet body, her non-body, as more ragdoll than
real, fling-able, push-able, able to be subject to aggression.
So, her first thought is: do it. Come for me. Here I am. And
she even types that: do it. But then she unsends it before
he sees it and decides she doesn't like thinking of actual

Montreal IT man in her closet, that imagining him with the kind of knife that has a wooden handle and closes in on itself was too much. It made her want an actual date with an actual man in an actual bar on an actual Wednesday. Or better yet, it made her want to be entirely alone lying in her childhood bedroom, overhearing her mom talk about protesting a nearby trafficway slated to plunge through sacred wetlands.

She got up from the computer and checked the closet and then checked the bathroom, a few paces away. Her place was so small, and the mattress directly on the floor, so there was nowhere else to check. She logged out of all her social media, disconnected her laptop from Wi-Fi, and unplugged it from the wall, as if any of that did anything. She put into a bag all the clothes in her small closet that were rarely worn, the patent red boots she'd found at a thrift store, the pink jumpsuit she got at a tag sale in someone's open garage, the many similar-looking vintage handbags with their clanking Bakelite handles, the 1960s leopard coat, all the clothes and things that could make her people she'd thought she'd be but ultimately never was. She took the bag outside and set it on the curb, then climbed back up three floors, plugged her laptop in, reconnected to Wi-Fi, and looked for places to move. Spokane, Bellingham, Vancouver.

On Friday, Frida and Kyle set out without a plan. They walked, and Kyle ranted about the way humans didn't deserve dogs. Frida had no idea where this was coming from, but she let her go on.

Things like, "The way people train dogs to do all these tricks. I mean, why?" And: "People just leave them in cars! Or tied to trees! We should release them. For real. We should."

Kyle's silver hair was piled in a top knot, the kind Frida had never been able to achieve, and she had one of her cameras on a rainbow strap around her neck. It was clear to Frida that Kyle was going to have an entirely different kind of life than the one Frida had.

You know how you can look at someone a lot of times, so many times, and you think you know the person? You think you've studied that face and could even draw it for some police sketch if it came to that, but then one day you're looking at the person and you notice something new, a freckle near an eyebrow, and maybe it wasn't there before, but probably it was. Will you tell me that thing?

When Frida was seventeen, the fall of her senior year, her mom took off with one of the garage men to drive to a community in the desert where people lived in their cars.

"The house is yours," Frida's mom had said, but when Frida herself left it a few weeks later, back door wide open, when she set the animals in their mudroom crates free, when she took off in the car her mother had abandoned, she didn't think about the way raccoons would ravage the house, the way squirrels would set up shop in her bedroom, the way mice would live and die in the kitchen, the way whatever had been hers or her about the place would be stripped away by so many creatures in so little time: vines, water, wind, birds flying in and panicking themselves to death against a wall or a window. People are erasable. Or, better yet, people are what we think they are at any given moment. Or if you want to get annoying about it, people are random assemblages of matter, ticking time bombs inching at every second toward disassembly, so catch them while you can, make of them what you will.

The first dog was easy. It was white and over-groomed and tied to a small tree in a planter. It licked Frida's whole arm when she went up to it, and then, when untied, hovered around her shins. Frida thought that maybe the dog loved its person, maybe it didn't want to go anywhere, maybe it would be worse off when it roamed away.

"Be free!" Kyle said. The dog looked around, not knowing. A newspaper on the bus bench next to them was open to an article whose headline read, "Visitor finds decapitated sea lions on California beach, discovery not as sinister as she thought."

Frida swore she saw a flash then of the man, the bookstore man, maybe the bar man, Montreal IT man, maybe, though she only saw the side of his face in the last picture he sent and couldn't fully connect the dots, but still, there it was, the sharp angle of his jaw, familiar, maybe. He waved at her, smiled in a way that made her freeze, made her turn away and pull Kyle closer to the building on their side of the street.

The white dog sniffed its own ass and trotted toward a trash can where it feuded with a couple of ravens before disappearing around a corner. The man, was he real, or had she imagined him? Regardless, he was gone, but there was something tipping point about it, like online Frida and real Frida had melded. She wanted to put herself in a cushioned box or to flail so much that nothing could get close. The fact was: nothing could really protect you.

The labradoodle they found and released next was easier. It knew immediately to start running. Then there was an Australian Shepherd (wanted petting before galloping down Haight), a Doberman mix (barked at everyone it passed), some kind of mutt that jumped up on people at random and knocked over a man in a suit who shouted, "fucking hound" over and over. Yes, some people yelled at Frida and Kyle as they disconnected dogs from their leashes, "What the fuck are you doing?" but just as many people ignored them completely. They lost track of how many dogs they released.

When they got to Stowe Lake, everyone was either walking a dog or petting a dog or both, and it felt like an embarrassment of riches. So many people with furry things feeling happy or generous, smiling at each other, nodding, the audacity of all of it.

Give me a big moment, a cymbal crash after a steam-gathering crescendo. Okay, what about this?

Kyle knelt to pet a chow tied to a post with no person expressing ownership nearby. There was no reason to think this dog would be any different, any less friendly, than all the other dogs. It wore a goddamned bandana. Kyle leaned down, and Frida held her breath. as if they were together reaching out some collective hand. Before she could exhale, the dog had bitten straight into several of Kyle's fingers. There was blood everywhere, and Kyle wasn't screaming or crying. Frida wondered: *was this blood or blood, like was this blood to worry about, hospital blood, or was this blood that could be assuaged with a band-aid?*

Blood is blood, she could imagine someone saying, and maybe that person was her mom with an opossum head or maybe it was the computer man as closet hologram holding a knife and maybe she invited him forward or shooed him away. *The mind,* Frida thought, *you can't fucking lose it.*

A man in a white shirt stopped jogging, took his shirt off, and wrapped it around Kyle's hand. "I'm a doctor," he said to them, and sure, great, that was good to have around, but did he have to be so show-offy about it?

"Cool," Kyle said, and Frida expected her to cry then, but she didn't. Instead, she started running. The white fabric around her hand turned red, and Frida was then pretty sure this was the kind of thing that would require special shots and an ER visit and probably stitches. But she followed Kyle anyway, running first and then walking, stopping eventually, out of breath, at a strip of stores with a nail place, a comic book shop, and a massage parlor papered over with lurid cartoony closeups of manicured hands on backs.

Why, Frida wondered, *given all the options for humanity, for growth, for community, was this the world we imagined for ourselves?*

Oil spills and food stains dotted the parking lot, and a man in nothing but leopard-print leggings and battered Air Force Ones sat on the sidewalk.

Kyle and Frida sat down near the man. Their phones were dinging and then ringing, but they didn't answer. *Did Kyle text her moms,* Frida wondered. She wasn't sure how the moms would know something was wrong, but they seemed like people who just knew things.

How was Frida to know that that winter would be the winter she'd meet someone, an actual person, fall as much as she was able to in love, get pregnant. She'd become a person who baked bread and stayed home with a baby, an actual living breathing human baby! She'd stand by a window and hold the baby while waiting for something. She would think about tracking down her own mother, about wandering desert tent cities until she found her so wild and rough that plants were growing from under her toenails. But she wouldn't. She'd wonder about the Internet men, about them as the chorus in a musical, tap dancing together and then being pulled by a long cartoon hook off stage. The apartment where she would stand with the baby would be warm from the radiators, and the baby would be asleep and practically purring on her shoulder, and it would be a good moment, a warm one, but she'd still be herself, that wouldn't have changed, and so the sidewalk or the clouds or someone hugging someone out the window would still make her sad for no reason, would still make her want to run. But she would have learned to sit it out, to stay, to touch and be touched and fuck and be fucked and sleep next to another body that might roll over and against her, and she would not always have to pull away.

For Kyle, all of it, her whole week with Frida, would be something interesting to tell people at some food truck festival or in a dorm room in Vermont or around the table at some dinner where they would drink medicinal-seeming cocktails and eat shrimp chips from a wire basket, as in "Once I ran all the way across San Francisco with my strange babysitter-nanny-person with my hand dripping blood while my moms stalked me and eventually showed up with the police."

A police car pulled into the parking lot, and the moms in a tiny blue Smart car were right behind.

Was everything okay? Was everything going to be okay? Tell me this was pivotal. Tell me it mattered. Tell me Frida would be different and better, with a brain less full of noise and better suited to post-modernity.

But there was nothing wrong, nothing really. Kyle and Frida were happy. A pack of dogs, racing, howling, tongues

lolling, synchronized in their mania, gleeful even, rounded
the corner. The moms were frantic, grabbing, leaning, and
there was a beauty to it, as if in this moment they could
secure Kyle, affix her to them, stop all the ways time was
going to come for them. Then the sun broke through.

Camp Heather

At sixty, Heather started working at a religious camp. No one else wanted the job, which involved monitoring boys who'd been sent by their parents to a place in southern Missouri that was supposed to, through insistence, deprivation, and repetition, turn them into Jesus people.

"You don't look like a Heather," the woman in the office told Heather when she walked in with her resume printed on a piece of paper, something she was sure most people didn't do anymore.

"All the Heathers are old now," Heather said. "None of us look like Heathers anymore."

The woman in the office did the kind of laugh that sounds like preparation for spitting.

When she was younger, Heather hadn't been one of the roller-skating Heathers or the skateboarding Heathers. She'd tucked no colorful plastic combs into back pockets. She'd slow danced in dark gyms with exactly no one.

The office woman led her to a screened cottage at the end of a path. Heather saw a ruler-length centipede scuttle under a cinderblock. The woman gave her two sets of starchy sheets. She gave her Crocs swirled in the camp's blue and yellow signature colors. She gave her a pillow stuffed too full and three t-shirts, each with a cartoon Jesus face on the front. She gave her a three-ring binder with lists of her job duties that could be summed up as: keep an eye on the six boys in Number Three, the cabin next to hers.

Heather had always thought God was a cruel trick, a filmy story about a beautiful afterlife invented to make people more comfortable with bearing horribleness on earth. As she'd gotten older, though, she'd felt religiousness would be nice. It would be nice to be able to imagine on the other side of all of this is a soft landing, a place with whatever you thought was the best waiting for you. What would those things be for her? Noodles cooked soft with cottage cheese and salt like her mother had given her when she was sick. Music she knew all the words to. Her sister, gone ten years. Flowers would be nice, but she didn't need them. Birds—their songs at least. She didn't have to see them flying to know they were there.

She walks to the camp's dining hall at the designated time. A few other grownups in the Jesus shirts greet her by the screen door. The door slaps closed like a shot. They introduce themselves. Miles. Lula. Martine. Sloane. Billie.

"Let me show you your table," Billie says and leads her back to a corner where six teenagers sit with heads lowered while a prayer blasts out of wall-mounted speakers. One of the six is mouthing words along with the prayer, but if Heather leans in, she can hear he's saying gibberish, nothing. The kid raises his eye, catches her staring, and mouths *Fuck* pause *off* and puts his head down again.

Heather had not had children. She'd dated someone through her thirties who told her repeatedly to wait and then wait and then wait. When she finally ended it with him, she was single and forty-five and rarely ovulated and couldn't imagine being a mother. She wasn't that remorseful, though. Her sister had three children, and it had engulfed her and aged her and made her, in the kids' early years, more boring and always tired.

When the prayer ends, the kids at the table pass rectangular plastic vats of food from person to person. Heather expected starchy food, fried things, but one container is full of tofu cubes feathered with pulverized cilantro, and the other tub is a grain she doesn't know the name of mixed with rangy protrusions of broccolini.

"The Vegans strike again," the Fuck Pause Off kid says. He stabs tofu chunks with a butter knife, lines up three of them up, and eats them in one animal bite. The kid to his right says, "Sigh," and the kid to his left says, "Jesus, get us some steak." Heather recognizes henchmen when she sees them.

Heather doesn't talk but gleans from their conversation that there are two different kitchen crews that change out every few days: The Meat People and The Vegans. In the open kitchen beyond her table, she sees cooks mix and chop on chrome tables. They wear paper bonnets and look taut and, she thinks, judgmental.

After dinner, they all gather in a padded, open-air gym and listen to a long acoustic guitar medley before a lecture from the camp's owner, Dan, who tells them he was a cocaine-addicted Division I football player who ended up almost dying on the field and saw a light. The henchmen move their hands in the air like "blah blah blah."

"This motherfucker again," Fuck Pause Off whispers. Sammy. His name is Sammy.

. The Vegans from the kitchen sit under a row of screenless windows at the edge of the gym and let mosquitoes go at their calves and forearms without swatting them. What Heather presumes to be The Meat People pace at the back of the gym. They look electrified. They scratch at things and wipe sweat from their faces and head bob when the music starts again.

In the middle of the night, Heather wakes up, goes to the kitchen, which is unlocked, cooks a steak on the flattop, and brings it back to her table's cabin with a bouquet of forks. She leaves it on the concrete floor, crunches her Crocs over stones back to her cabin, and wishes for a motion-activated camera so she could watch the meat smell waking them and how they would gather around the plate on the floor like six happy dogs.

In the morning, she gets up before her cabin kids do and goes down to the lake where they are supposed to meet before breakfast for a prayer at sunrise. The path to the water is dusty and narrow. Branches of things she can't identify in the half-dark scratch thin lines on her biceps.

Her phone beeps in her pocket, and it's one of her sister's kids, now thirty and pregnant, sending her a jokey photo of her bulbous stomach with a face drawn on it. Heather immediately has the old instinct of wanting to text her sister, to say something like, "Your kid is so pregnant," but, of course, her sister is gone, and that can be a fresh hurt even ten years later. Heather can remember being a kid with her sister and racing cars in the flat creek bed in front of their apartment or making biospheres for snails in glass jars that had held pasta sauce. Adulthood has gone so much faster than childhood, really, and the memories she has of it feel flat and like they belong to someone else.

Heather sits on the dock, sets the Crocs next to her, and lets her feet hang in the dark water. She doesn't hear Dan come onto the dock, but when he puts a flat palm on her head, she almost falls over into the water.

"Morning," he says, and then, "Didn't mean to startle you," but she thinks he probably did.

He's close to her age, but his arm muscles appear intact and unchanged from whatever they were thirty years before. He wears a shirt with the sleeves cut off that says *in his name!* in cursive across the front. She thinks he's actively flexing.

"Don't mind me," he says. He drinks from a metal water bottle, but when he pulls it away, his lips are rimmed with dots of blueberries.

"You have," she makes a gesture with her hand around her mouth and then trails off, and he wipes his forearm across his mouth and then leans down to dunk his whole arm in the lake water. It makes Heather think of the parts and pieces of people flung everywhere. His spit and blueberry residue and DNA floating in the water. Her hairs or skin flakes or eyelashes back in Kansas City or Lawrence or Denver or any one of the places she's lived. Her sister knitted into zinnias or rolled around the rubber of a car tire.

It only takes a minute for the sky to undo itself completely. It goes from an impenetrable teal to stripey and shot through with peach and fuchsia. The kids are then thick on the path with their gruff morning noises.

They gather on the dock, against which a giant inflated plastic pillow they call the blob gurgles. The blob is a doublewide-sized slab under a diving platform that the camp kids spend late afternoons lofting themselves off and then splatting onto the blue and yellow inflated fabric before sliding off and under the opacity of the lake.

Dan says to the crowd of teenagers and the counselors in huddles at their periphery, "Control is an illusion. I want to believe you are all smart enough to know this. You think you're in control when you're doing these things. Taking the money. Swallowing a pill. Doing a line." Heather can tell Dan feels smug and powerful for having done some of the same things these teenagers have gotten in trouble for doing. Unlike her sister, Heather had never done anything. She was the person home during the parties. It hadn't bothered her, though, not really, at least. She'd told herself that engagement with life didn't have to be the kind that could be loud and recognizable by bystanders. Still, she often felt kept apart. Wrapped in cardboard. She'd camped in a hundred national parks. She'd sat at dusk and watched a coyote and a moose skirmish over something. The moose reared up on its back legs, and the coyote, low to the ground but still believing in its power, kept approaching, and the moose turned and ran. She was the moose, maybe. Or maybe she wasn't the moose or the coyote but some tusk-colored bird, lurking.

The six boys in the cabin she's in charge of stand in a cluster on the dock. Sammy rolls his eyes, and Andre does the jacking-off hand motion, and Kai covers his face with his hand, and Chas yawns, and BB looks off into the middle distance, and Rain is a statue and maybe asleep with his eyes open.

"Let me tell you, though," Dan says. His calf muscles twitch with intention. "You're not in control." Dan reaches his arm out and knocks BB into the water. Then Rain, then Chas. The three of them, stunned, flap and gasp for a minute before regaining their composure and making their way to the ladder hanging off the side of the dock.

"What in the actual fuck," BB says and wipes water from his eyes. Chas shakes himself off like a retriever. Rain stamps on the dock and coughs.

"Exactly," Dan says.

A heron decimates a fish on the beach beyond the dock. A bell clangs. Heather smells potatoes cooking with rosemary. The boys pulse and breathe and sigh and sweat. The morning is hot already, and it's vibrating with possibility. Heather wants to wake up each morning thinking it matters, wants to look in corners for the things that on that day will make her feel swollen with being, but more often than she wants to admit, she feels pulled down into grayness, into a zipper of time with each notch screaming to her: *there goes some* and *there goes some more*.

The peaches and pinks fade from the sky. Dan says, "Okay, breakfast," and the boys rustle, and make their way off the dock, up the path, and to the dining hall.

Sammy, pills, check fraud. Andre, light hacking. Chas, cocaine. Kai, vandalism, targeted harassment. Rain, repeated shoplifting. BB, just vodka.

So boring, all their infractions. All the expected ones.

"Yawn," Heather practices saying in the warped mirror above her dresser. "Tell me something new." In case they do, in fact, tell her, which they don't. Though, when, after eleven o'clock, she sits cross-legged on the stones in the dark behind their cabin, the stones turning her thighs as textured as crocodile skin, she hears them.

"That woman is creepy," Sammy says.

"So creepy," Andre says.

"Why couldn't we get a Billie. Number Four has a Billie," Sammy says.

"The Billie tits!" Kai says.

"They could have been ours, our tits, the tits of Number Three," Chas says.

"Like mascots," BB says.

"Or when Billie's wearing that sports bra, mascot, singular," Rain says, and the cabin goes quiet for a minute.

Sammy laughs and says, "Rain, dude, you're fucking hilarious."

Heather goes back inside her cabin, dons all three of her sports bras, one over the other, until she's flattened, and her breath is shallow. She eats the whole bag of sour balls she'd bought at a gas station on the way to the camp. She finds a pen on the desk, draws a cartoony face on her stomach, snaps a picture of it. In the dark with the phone camera flash, her skin looks waxen. She sends the picture to her sister's kid, and her sister's kid immediately *ha ha's* it. Heather pulls the scratchy sheet over her chin, leaves her tongue unbrushed and coated in sugary sour syrup, and goes to sleep.

The Meat People, it turns out, are wealthy. New money people. Boats, lake houses. Waistband bags with recognizable logos. "They cook not for the money," Billie tells her when they walk into the dining hall, "but for the sheer love of the food." Heather hears the word Wagyu rolling out from the kitchen more than once when they prepare what they call, without self-consciousness, The Weekend Feast. She's embarrassed for them and misses the angled austerity of The Vegans.

The rectangular table vats are, on Weekend Feast Day, filled with expensive cuts of meat cooked perfectly. Heather has never loved meat. She'd not gone so far as to swear it off completely, but she's never liked the feel of it in her teeth. She can't stop thinking of it as animal when she's eating. The boys, however, go crazy for it.

"Weekend Feast for the win," Sammy says.

"So fucking good," BB says.

"The sweet relief of not a vegetable in sight," Chas says.

"I can and will empty that container," Rain says.

"Bro, fight me for it," Andre says.

"Settle down, my dudes, The Meat People will bring more," Kai says.

Heather eats a bite or two and sets down her fork and knife. To the boys, she is not there, and that makes the job easier. It's a choice to remain untouchable and thus unscathed, though the boys would likely claim it's something they put on her. When she stands and walks the pebble path to the cabin, scoops one of the centipedes into a bucket before it can scuttle from her, and puts it under the sheets of the bunk she knows to be Sammy's, she says out loud into the empty cabin, "Only a ghost can do that."

Every day is sports. In the morning, after breakfast, they run from the dining hall to the upper fields by the road where they divide into groups to play soccer or football or baseball or basketball. Heather is better at running than she assumed she would be. The boys are sweating and, after weeks of this solid activity, no longer have body fat. Midmorning, they go to the pool or the lake to swim or dive or sail. It's not unusual for someone to faint from lack of water and the heat and exertion, to drop on the trail between the fields and the lake, but when Sammy does, Heather knows it's going to change things for him, affect his leadership spot, make him fallible. The other boys of Number Three run ahead. Heather pulls Sammy up to sitting and holds him on a dusty boulder until his eyes uncross and he drinks the water from her plastic bottle.

"I didn't need help," he says.

"You did," she says.

"I would have been fine."

The other boys are long gone to hurl themselves onto the blob or be pulled on a rope behind a boat.

"Why are you here anyway?" Sammy says.

"I'm not sure," she says. She can see from the way he holds himself, the way his hands are unmarred, that he has grown up without a thought that food might not be in the refrigerator when he opens it in the morning, and that is the case for every boy here.

The Vegans pass on the path above, moving from the parking lot to the dining hall. They carry cloth bags full of food and say things like "Pleasant morning" and "Another wonderful day by the lake," but she has decided they are secretly cynical and brooding. Maybe they smoke cigarettes while sitting on buckets behind the dining hall and have made up cruel, punishing nicknames for all of them.

"Will you leave after our six weeks?" Sammy asks. Six weeks is what it's supposed to take to make the camp kids better and righteous, to fling them back in the directions of their parents, polished and devout and imbued with absolution.

"I'll probably stay for the next group. There's one more before closing for the fall."

"And then what?"

It was always that in life. The line of it unfurling. And then. And then. She could see it as relentless or beautiful. Every *I will* casting the boat forward and forward some more. Dan, the camp owner, was right, though, the boat was mainly going to keep proceeding, and Heather couldn't stop it. Some people would stop it, like her sister, but Heather never had been and never would be one of those people, and maybe instead of the defeat she'd once thought that was, that was a victory, or maybe it didn't matter what she called it or how she thought of it because no matter, her boat, whether she sat or stood or screamed or sighed or watched or wavered or wondered or closed her goddamned eyes, was still moving.

When Sammy stands, his legs are, again, steady. He looks at her like he doesn't know her and takes off on the path running.

On the boys' last day, they are supposed to eat breakfast, hang out by the lake without the pressure of planned sports, and then come together for a final dinner at Dan's house.

At breakfast, Heather tries to talk to them about the future.

"She speaks," Andre says.

"We were all beginning to wonder," Chas says.

She tells them Dan was right about almost nothing, but he was right about control. She tells them things they don't expect will come for them, will happen, and they'll have no choice but to get around those things and to the other side.

"Profound," Andre says and laughs.

"Bro," BB says, and they all stop talking.

They eat the rest of the apricot muffins and egg bites. The Vegans said they are free of animal products. They don't just eat. They gnaw and shovel and spray crumbs and leave a mess.

When they leave the dining hall, Heather follows a few body lengths behind them, down to the dock. The trees titter and bend. The water ruffles and slaps itself against the wood. Heather sits behind a motorboat. The boys pull the giant yellow and blue blob over close enough to the dock that they can jump on. They grab onto the plastic handles on the blob when their shifting weight destabilizes it. Then they sit in a circle of compressed plastic at the blob's middle, so Heather can hear them, but she can't see them.

"It's weird but I kind of don't want to leave," Andre says.

"Dude, come on," Sammy says.

"Home sounds awful right now. I get it," Kai says.

"But the drugs!" Chas says. He's laughing, but also, he means it.

Heather wraps her arms around her chest. The day is colder than the previous day, an unexpected snap.

"My girlfriend sent me a nude, so I'm packed and ready," Rain says.

The wind makes the water look like textured frosting.

"Yo," BB says. "I hear that."

"I can't believe it's almost August," Andre says.

"Sophomore year, baby," Sammy says.

"I wouldn't mind going backwards," Kai says. "Like ninth grade all over again."

"Don't be a wuss, man," Chas says. "This year is going to be fire."

Then they go quiet, and Heather assumes they are leaning back, closing their eyes, waiting for it to be tomorrow when their parents will ferry them back to whatever big houses they've spent their childhoods in.

Heather unties the ropes that connect the blob to the dock without any of the boys noticing. Their weight in the center means they are a bit buried by the uptick of the plasticky fabric on all sides.

The wind takes the blob away from the dock quickly before any of them realizes it's moving. Sammy is the first to sit up. Heather sees a flash of his face. She's not sure, but she thinks it looks slightly stricken.

The blob moves farther into the lake. She worries she's done the wrong thing, but then she hears the boys not screaming, but laughing. To them, being loosed onto the wide lake is nothing but more glee. They leap and do dramatic flips off the side. They hold onto the plastic handles and hoist themselves back up and slip off and climb again.

Heather thinks she should be somehow incited to action by this, by everything, that she should be the kind of person who runs up the path to her cabin, gets her backpack, starts her car, and drives north away from the camp, past all the racist yard flags that remind her what southern Missouri is really about, all the way to the house of her sister's kid, where she could knock on the door and maybe hold in her arms the baby that will look nothing like her sister, where she could whisper some perfectly profound thing to this baby, a series of words that would lodge like a seed in the baby's brain and somehow sustain the baby for years.

Instead, Heather lays on the dock and tries to make her mind the blank nothing that meditation experts say is the goal. She stays like that until the boys start to make their way back in. They hold the blob's ropes and swim the blob through the water back toward the dock. They're red and winded. When they get it back into position, Sammy reties all the ropes.

"Oh my god, you fucking got us, *Heather*," Sammy says and drips water all over her as he shakes out his hair.

"Classic Heather," Rain says. They stand in a circle around her, and it feels more menacing than jovial. She walks to the ladder that leads up to the diving platform. A few months ago, she would not have imagined herself standing in this place.

The camp boys stomp on the dock and chant her name. She sees all the Heathers then, the people she could have been but wasn't, the roller-skating Heather, the comb-in-back-pocket Heather, easy in the middle of a group of teenagers. The mother Heather cutting apple slices in the kitchen when the sky is still dark. The wife Heather asking her husband something boring about school forms. The sister Heather who shows up at the right time on the right day to keep the bad thing from happening.

The boys are behind her on the ladder. She steps onto the platform. Her t-shirt balloons in the wind. She jumps. The coated fabric when she hits the blob envelops her completely, and in that moment, she's a happy baby. There are no what-ifs or could-have-beens.

That night, the last night for the boys, they go down a path through the forest to Dan's house, which is palatial. There are so many decks, and the kitchen alone is as big as any apartment Heather has lived in. The Vegans and The Meat People stand on opposite sides of a kitchen island that's long like a runway. It's a house that fits a hundred people.

Dan's wife is leaning back against the kitchen cabinets holding a plastic champagne flute. She is what Heather thought she would be. Face made taut by injectables and Botox but not in a way that makes her look thirty, more in a way that makes her look like a frozen waffle version of an unfrozen waffle.

"You must be Heather," Dan's wife says to her. "I'm Cindy." Another dying name. "Dan says you're a hoot," and Heather doesn't know what to make of this because she's said maybe ten words to Dan. Still, there's something about Cindy she immediately likes. Heather can tell she's also a watcher.

The family room attached to the kitchen has a wall of windows, and the upper ones are moons and half circles. The sunset over the lake is all purples. Bruises and mussel shells and undereye circles and the grape tomatoes The Vegans roll around in their palms, ready.

A piece of gold duct tape runs down the center of the kitchen island. The Vegans are in wide linen pants and wispy tank tops. The Meat People wear '80s metal band t-shirts, black pants, and boots, and their hair is unclean. They all seem to have a singularity of purpose, a hard focus to drill out all distractions. Heather can't remember the last time she had something that turned the head noise down to zero so she could roll through a series of invigorating and all-consuming tasks.

"Okay," Dan says, "Let's settle this! We'll see who can make the best food! Here we go!" he says, and Cindy blows a whistle, and the kitchen is bustle and noise.

The food they make! The Vegans start with a curry with carrots and potatoes and tomatoes and garam masala and cauliflower and coconut milk, and it bubbles in a pot that could fit two toddlers. They move on to papery-cut sweet potatoes and cashew gorgonzola and candied almonds and the most delicate and inoffensive shreds of kale. They hum while they cook, and it's orchestral. The Meat People trash talk and chant and make thin strips of crispy pork and chicken rubbed with dry fresh chili peppers and oil and a textbook beef Wellington. The Vegans build a layered pastry gleaming with raspberries, and no one believes it's made without butter. The Meat People churn out bacon brittle ice cream, and they all spoon it into each other's mouths without any concern for decorum. At the end, no one can agree on a winner, and after much debate they go out to the beach at the bottom of the deck stairs and stand in a circle as Dan builds a bonfire.

"This was actually kind of dope," Andre says.

"I mean...okay, dude," Sammy says.

"For real, though," Kai says.

"I'm always down for some killer food," Chas says.

"Like, who isn't?" Rain says.

"Facts," BB says.

Dan turns on a projector, and a twenty-foot video Jesus hovers on the top of the lake. It's not old-school Jesus in robes. This Jesus wears a blue tracksuit with gold stripes but still has the hair and beard and soft, forgiving face of the white Jesus from every crucifixion painting in every Catholic school. The tree leaves at the edge of the water are illuminated, though, and the beauty of their outlines against the water almost makes Heather cry.

"Oh my god, what the actual fuck," Andre says, and he's laughing, pointing at tracksuit Jesus.

"Hahaha, so funny," Sammy says.

"This fucking guy," Kai says, and looks over at Dan who sits in a yellow Adirondack chair and folds his hands over his stomach like an actual king.

These boys will remember this, Heather knows, but they won't be changed. They'll go right back to whatever it was they were before. They'll be frat boys or high-functioning alcoholics or finance bros or middle-aged dads dreaming of high school.

"You should stay," Dan's wife says to her, and Heather knows it is in part because she, Heather, is unthreatening. Still, it is something to be wanted. Heather has had a life-time of holding herself apart from everyone, and it's left her blank and sad.

"We have work in the winter," Cindy says, "It's different, but it's still work." Cindy leans back in one of the chairs and folds her hands into her lap and lets out the kind of sigh that seems like it might deflate her completely. Heather can't tell if it's dissatisfaction or contentment.

Heather thinks of what winter there would be: rabbits on the lake ice. Eagles showing off in swoops overhead. A fox-tail moving between birch trees. Maybe she'd meet someone in town, and together they'd walk the perimeter of the lake and leave boot tracks in the snow. There's nothing really for Heather to run to or toward. Her sister now is more and more something she cannot conjure. Some remembered words. A voice. The day before, her sister's daughter, a few hours away in Kansas City, had sent her a video clip of the new baby, a girl with her sister's name. Alicia.

The boys drag branches to the fire, and it gets as tall as lake Jesus. The crackling reminds Heather of all the good things about childhood, being warm under covers at night, having someone come in then to tell you everything's good, everything will be okay.

The Meat People and The Vegans have coalesced around the fire pit. There's not the animosity Heather presumed there would be. Instead, there's back slapping and even full-body hugging. Heather thinks about putting herself in the middle of that group of bodies, of the beautiful methodi-cal-ness of, say, scraping a hundred carrots or deveining that many shrimp. A person could get happily, fully lost in that.

"Seriously," Cindy says, "Stay. It will be great." Cindy reaches a hand out and lands it on Heather's leg for a second the way a bee might land on you while on its way to something brighter.

"Okay," Heather says. Maybe she will.

People's Parties

On the last day of ninth grade, Beatrice found herself at a rooftop party in The Mission. It wasn't the kind of thing she normally did: friends, groups, music. Someone was playing "Jessie's Girl" on repeat, and people in gold tennis shoes and embroidered bomber jackets and overalls were dancing and hugging and then dancing again.

It was a moment. Beatrice could appreciate it from a distance: the irony and the glee all wrapped together like a snow globe that someone kept shaking and shaking. After thirty minutes, she went down through the roof hatch, down the spiral staircase, and into the apartment owned by the boy having the party. The boy, Frederick, was a junior, and both his dads did something in tech, and it was clear they cared about their apartment. Heath pottery in careful stacks on the raw wood kitchen shelves. A charcoal velvet couch, the requisite art books in towers. Hanging plants on delicate wires make a garden out of every window.

Bea's hair was long with the bottom inches of the brown dyed black, and that morning she'd let her grandmother,

Wendy, cut bangs that had immediately developed a mind of their own. She'd had to shellac them with coconut oil before leaving her house. She assumed they would elicit a forehead-wide patch of acne.

There was this presumed promiscuity of everyone Bea's age. Her mom's friends liked to talk about it in the way of, "Bea, I'm sure all your friends are hooking up already, so be careful." One: she didn't really have friends. Two: no one had so much as kissed her, and she was mainly fine with that.

So it was with caution, disbelief, and oblivion that she met Frederick's attention. In the two dads' bedroom, beneath the noise of the party, she'd hidden out on a corner loveseat with the door to the bedroom almost closed and made a show of flipping through a Vivian Maier book to seem occupied, should anyone venture down from the roof. She had practiced staying off her phone on such occasions. She didn't want to be one of those girls always on her phone.

Frederick's progress was slow: first peeking in the bedroom and giving her a wave, then making an ice water in the kitchen (she heard the clatter and plunk), then returning to the bedroom, pointing and laughing at his Bernie shirt onto which he'd markered "I told you so," then clicking the door closed, and picking up another art book (William Eggleston) and still not saying anything, then sitting on the edge of the bed and saying one thing while looking down ("Sick pictures. Totally relevant, still") and then a full thirty seconds later looking up to see if Bea was listening or looking, then sitting beside her but separated by inches of fabric for a half hour of parallel reading before he really went in. She could practically feel the weight of people's feet on the roof above them, but the music was muffled by the closed windows and door. He was so quick, and she was so unsuspecting that she couldn't find her voice. Instead, she stared for those few minutes at the open Vivian Maier book that had fallen on the floor, at one bleak and disarming picture of an elderly woman in a hair net and a fur coat, the sun making its spotlight a dagger on the fur, and the woman's face saying to Bea: this is all your fault.

Later that night in the bathroom of the house she shared with her mother, she used a pair of kids' safety scissors and a pink plastic razor to disarm her head of all its hair. She slept with two ragged stuffed animals pressed into either side of her face and did her best from the following morning forward to pretend the night had never happened.

The houseboat is full of women, many of them draped in ponchos from other continents. Ray, in a yellow '60s coat-dress and gold clogs, leans into her girlfriend, Chantal, on a giant sheepskin in the houseboat's central room. Through the boat's front window, Ray sees her daughter Beatrice sitting on the front railing and reading *The New York Review of Books* under an outdoor light. The party—Chantal's fortieth—is a mix of vegan appetizers, Tequila rickeys, and an improvised game of Trivial Pursuit.

When Ray slept with anyone anymore, it was with women. She'd learned she preferred it, the tits, the sway, the languidness. She was a small woman, bony and short, and she was attracted to big women. In the past ten years, her friend group had morphed from moms she knew through Bea's various Montessori and Waldorf schools to a handful of exes and their exes who gathered for endless Friday night dinners.

Ray had finished an architecture degree in the mid-90s
and had at the time many ideas about communal and portable housing. She'd spent a summer in Malawi building
structures out of reclaimed materials and helping a Scot-
tish guy install solar panels in clinics. In the second half
of her twenties, she scrapped it all and played with a band
whose punkish skater singer appealed to a large number
of disgruntled white boys. She'd slept with many of them,
and one of them was Bea's father.

The first year of motherhood was unbearable. Ray's own
mother, Wendy, a musician, a nomad who had raised Ray
in a series of VW vans and friends' places up and down the
north coast, had vanished a month before Bea was born
and only resurfaced after Bea's tenth birthday.

Ray spent Bea's first year living in one room in a basement near The Mission. She and Bea slept on a single mattress. Her music friends didn't understand her or wanted
nothing to do with her. One night one of them brought
her a puppy ("I thought it would cheer you up," he said)
and Ray, out of her mind with sleeplessness, let the dog
out the window and onto the sidewalk before sunrise and
never saw it again. Ray, ripped open by insomnia, pushed
a screaming or sleeping Bea down all the sidewalks late
at night. Once, after midnight, a stumbling man in gold
pants stopped, pulled down his shining pants, and peed
into the open stroller, right onto Bea's blanket. There was
nothing more alone-feeling than being alone outside with
an infant at two A.M. When Bea turned one, Ray got her
into a HeadStart daycare and found a temp gig at an architecture firm where she eventually worked her way up to
designing kitchens for tech industry moms who all wanted
the same thing but swore they were nonconformist.

Chantal's houseboat kitchen was a jungle. The butcher's block table under the window was covered entirely by plants, their tendons spilling over the wood. Plants hung from the ceiling in macramé hangers, and Chantal had so much jasmine that the smell gave Ray a headache. Chantal kept a watering record on a wall calendar with tiny checkmarks, one for each plant, "because they know if I don't check them off," she'd once told Ray. Ray's childhood had made her distrust magical thinking of all kinds, but Chantal was the mother she'd never had: soft, a hugger, someone Bea would actually speak to even when she wasn't speaking to Ray.

At the end of Chantal's party, a large boat passes too close in the bay, and the houseboat rocks as if it's out on open water. One stoneware dish full of picked-over wrapped figs slides off the table and crashes onto the floor where it takes on the look of carnage. The glass of red wine Ray is holding sloshes up onto her dress. Bea comes in the sliding door. A few years before, Ray and Bea had watched a documentary about a teenaged girl who sailed around the world by herself, and Ray remembers Bea wanting so badly to be that girl.

The water smooths out, and the boat settles. The women help clean the broken plate and then gather their bags and scarves. Ray looks down and sees what looks like a South America stain of red wine traveling down the front of her dress. Chantal kisses Ray's cheek. They make a plan for dinner the next day, and Bea and Ray are out the door.

After forty, Ray had donated almost all her clothes, anything patterned or fussy, and started from scratch, scavenging at various thrift stores. She'd put together a few monochromatic uniforms, and she cycled through them every week. And she'd stopped watching men. She'd stopped reacting to their reactions to her. She'd reached an under-standing of their fundamental envy of women. It was a relief not to care about them anymore.

On the way back down to the city, Ray drives slowly over the bridge. "Remember that movie about the girl on the sailboat," Ray says to Bea, and Bea says nothing but nods and points out to the water where there appear to be hun-dreds of boats of all sizes, their lights creating broad yellow planets on the water around them. It is like this with them now, and Ray finds herself giddy in these allowed moments of connection. She grabs Bea's hand, and Bea, for several whole seconds, does not pull away.

Even though she had once written a famous song that wrapped 1970s love in a package to hand out to teenagers in Iowa and Vermont and North Dakota, Wendy doesn't play music anymore. She is seventy and has lost her voice to smoking, and her fingers hate the guitar.

Instead, she wakes early and before heading to the beach to meet her daughter and granddaughter, she walks the neighborhood for at least an hour wearing massive gold headphones, a gift from her granddaughter, Beatrice. She traverses the blocks to the beach, by all the noodle shops, the men smoking by trash cans, the ravens carving meals out of discarded plastic food containers, the trains ziplining their clatter down streets' centerlines. The whole neighbor-hood weighted with fog and metal feels poised to slip off into the water. She missed the entire first decade of being a grandmother, and she's played her best catch-up since returning to the city.

Like all the mornings in the Outer Sunset, it is foggy. The usual swimming men sit near the water on their usual blanket, the one with a picture of a growling bear that looks 3D and almost velvet. As she does every Saturday, Wendy watches as the swimming men sit through a few final moments of observation before being stripped to nothing by the cold ocean water. The beach is uncrowded and chilly. There are a few teenagers camped out under a shelter built of driftwood and towels. A group of mothers with children in layers of fleece try repeatedly to light candles on a birthday cake, but the wind keeps taking the flame, and then one of the kids scoops the center out of the cake and shoves the yellow into his mouth. Wendy hums low under her breath, a seashell tone, and looks at where water and sky come together in a gray line crosshatched by gulls and pelicans.

The swimming men rest metal coffee mugs on their bare stomachs. In nothing but their swimming trunks and with the bellies of men years past middle age, they look pregnant. They are all her age, in that gauzy time of life when caring about others' opinions becomes less consequential. She has heard women complain about their invisibility after sixty, as in "No one even notices me anymore," but Wendy delights in it. She loves the un-bodying of it, the way she can walk around undetected sometimes in the way of a wind or a spirit. She wears whatever she wants. Sometimes she doesn't respond at all when a man asks her a question but holds his stare before turning away.

She watches as the bulldozer operators, three of them about a hundred yards down the beach, move and flatten the sand. Under her bed, she has a box that contains three records she made in her twenties, all with photos of her on the cover: one with hair to her waist standing in a field, smoking, another of her lying on a bed with a scarf over her breasts, and another where she floats on her back with a daisy behind each ear in a perfect '60s LA pool. When she thinks back on that time, she can only remember her physical self, the body, but she can't remember what it felt like to be that person.

The bulldozer operators take a break and gather by the steps, circulating a flask. They drink and then lean against the retaining wall where someone has spray painted "Deport Trump" in rainbow bubble letters and an abstract monkey in purple shouting: "Bananas for the People!" The sun makes a line on the beach and quickly disappears.

She sees her daughter and granddaughter on the steps. Her daughter is all in white like Yoko Ono. Her once-black hair is now half gray and in braids. Bea's newly short hair is covered in a thick black wool hat, and she looks in all directions in the way of a mouse spotted out in the open by a human.

This is their Saturday ritual now. Ray brings an old-timey picnic basket with her and positions herself cross-legged on a blanket next to Wendy so that she never really has to look at her. They are still in this holding pattern wherein Ray tolerates Wendy, and they never talk of the past. Bea lies on her stomach and eats peanut butter and honey toast, the peanut butter leaving prints on her cheeks that she doesn't bother to wipe away. Life astounds Wendy in a gut-punch way. The fact that she sits each Saturday on the beach with her tiny family of women she didn't know much at all five years before, no matter what the conflict or complications, is something.

When the swimming men set down their coffees and run to the water, their legs look part amphibian and part cadaver. The seagulls guffaw and scatter. The pastel houses hang on the cliff, almost but not entirely grayed out by the fog, and the green edge of the park carves a straight line into the flipped-ribbon chaos of the city.

The way the swimming men run without care is beautiful to Wendy. She never runs like that anymore, can't remember having run like that for years, but on this day, she gets up and runs right after them to the edge of the water. It's alive with shiny discarded mussels and fragmented crab shells. She backs away and watches the swimming men's legs as the water takes over their bodies, and then she herself drops down face down into the sand, burrows herself full length in until she has sand even in her teeth. When she hears her granddaughter yelling her name, she stands up and turns around, and there is Beatrice, shoes off and running through the sand. When she reaches her, Beatrice, though fifteen, jumps up into her arms like a baby.

Doctor Visit

You have the tiniest little baby cataracts, the ophthalmologist tells me, and he laughs, because apparently, cataracts, when small, are funny. I'm in the chair with the thing that looks like a 1970s TV robot hovering in front of my face and I don't think it's funny because 1) all I can imagine is my eyes becoming increasingly cloudy and unusable and 2) cataracts are in most cases a final-third-of-life thing or at least indication you've stopped walking on a path and are now on the stairs, and who knows how many stairs there will be, but you're on the stairs.

I should mention that we are fucking, the ophthalmologist and me—not in the office, but as a routine. And with some brutality, because I've never had patience for sex that is soft. Even though he's divorced, and I'm divorced, we don't fuck in beds. We meet. Cars on farm roads. Bathrooms of chain stores. Basements of open houses. Once in a corn maze at a pumpkin patch. It's always quick and fleeting, no lounging on comforters after, and thus a reminder about life and how it's easier but worse to hold yourself out, to stay cloudy and beyond harm.

When I was three, my dad's extended family drove in one of those long 1960s cars all the way to California. My dad's brother-in-law drove most of the way, and my dad's sister was on the right side of the car's long bench seat with the baby between them. My dad's parents sat in the back seat with my dad's sister's toddler climbing over them every now and then to press a cheek against the car's back windows. It was the first time my dad's parents, both poor and Midwestern, had been out of the state of Missouri. My dad was home in the middle of the country when they reached California, climbed down from the road to the water, and stood on a rock formation by the ocean when a wave bigger than the usual waves came up entirely over the rocks. The car was left at the top of the cliff above the path down among the rocks, and it was days before anyone figured out they were gone.

This is something I think about: mattering. As in, do we matter? It's a masturbatory thought exercise that undoes itself, as in, the sheer act of thinking about mattering is enough to remind you of the futility of your actions and thus proof you don't, in fact, matter, and why should mattering matter anyway? But in a practical sense, it's easy to find you do, in moments of immediacy, matter, like fucking in a car on a farm road when the act wouldn't be happening in that way without your essential contribution. But then, also, it could be someone else. Someone without baby cataracts.

"You can get surgery," the ophthalmologist says when I'm peeling my legs off the vinyl exam chair, and there's an actual ripping sound. "When it gets worse, you can get surgery. It hurts, but then they're gone." And maybe that sums up everything: it hurts, but then it's gone.

◆

The posters that cover the walls of my dermatologist's office tell me all the ways my face is wrong. It should look less aware of the world and its problems so that people looking at me will not feel alarmed by the ways my face is revealing the passage of time.

"I don't need to change my face," I tell the dermatologist, and it strikes me that there is not much in the office: a light on a metal leg with an arm that allows it to move at any angle, a cabinet likely full of utilitarian things like cotton swabs and bandages.

"But," the dermatologist says, and he swings the light so it's right in front of my nose, and I close my eyes. "This area," he says and pokes at the lines on my forehead between my two eyes, "could be better."

I open my eyes and lean away from the light and see his face, ruddy and wrinkled in the standard middle-aged-white-man way, but maybe it would be even more ruddy and wrinkled if he hadn't done all the things the posters in his office tell me I should do.

I should mention that we are fucking, the dermatologist and me—not in the office, but as a routine. I am divorced, and he is divorced, and the sex is acrobatic and strange, and sometimes when we are on the balcony of his apartment and it's two A.M. and my leg is up on the railing and I'm doing some kind of yoga backbend that seems improbable but it's working, I wonder, *what is this life*, because I'm deep like that. No, ha, I'm really not. I'll be watching *Love Island* in ten minutes in his bed and trying to think of nothing. There are no nighttime birds around here, and I wish for them on those balcony nights, a caw or a flutter. There could be owls if we hadn't driven them away by turning their woods into rows of condos painted the colors of rainbow goldfish to convince us that the builders of this complex were not boring and didn't go for the uniformity of gray or beige or muddy green across the landscape.

When I was three, my father's extended family was driving home from church on Christmas Eve in one of those long, low cars of the 1960s, the kind that look slightly flattened by some kind of giant junkyard compactor. My dad wasn't with them because he had stopped believing in church, and, besides, they were a few towns away, and they didn't talk as much as they should. His mother was wearing a tiny dark green velvet hat, and it might have been the most scandalous thing she had ever done. His father had on his suit and a tie onto which his mother had embroidered a small yellow cross on the red silk that maybe wasn't real silk but looked shiny and smooth. His sister was losing some of her hair early, and she combed it in a certain way that looked slightly off but that covered that patch at the back, and her two kids were in the car, one in the front, the other in the back, and her husband was the best driver, but he could not have anticipated the car that crossed over, coming around a curve on the last stretch before they would have dropped my father's parents back at their house. Cars were heavier then, and this meant both potential for protection and damage, and no one wore seat belts, which meant both freedom and lack of safety. Nothing was just one thing. My father got the call on Christmas morning, and we were opening presents of which my sister and I each had a few and they were things like sweaters and notebooks, and he dropped the wall phone so that it dangled and hit against the kitchen cabinet, and he walked out to the backyard—a square of grass, and if all that sounds dramatic, then, yes, it was.

This is something I think about: upkeep, as in, slowing the roll, face serums in tiny jars and backyard oases instead of tallgrass and bathroom remodels and intermittent fasting and dip manicures and the best sale ever on jeans that will make your ass pop. As in, on some days it seems like I should lie on my bed and not get up at all because eventually I will be lying down and not getting up anyway and my face will, if I'm lucky, be very wrinkled because I will be one of the ones who was allowed to get very old and to even have kids who have kids who have kids who will know bits of information about me even when I'm gone and say things like, She did xyz, and in their word capsules, I will have existed and will exist, and that is supposed to be something.

But for now, I pile the face cream thicker than maybe it's intended to be on the lines between my forehead while the dermatologist says, "It's a miracle worker, trust me," and I think of him on his balcony without pants, and I want to say: will it make me happy, will it help me sleep more than three hours at a time, will it teach me not to relive every conversation I ever have over and over, convinced I've said and done all the wrong things, will it cure cancer and end world hunger and stop men with guns and halt the forest fires and keep the volcanos from erupting and roll the planet back to what it was before people and cars or forward to what it should be. I walk out of the office with the white swath of expensive cream still visible on my skin.

Make me pretty. Make me better. Take me home.

My breast is a practically detachable slab of meat smashed between two walls of glass, and it doesn't hurt as much as everyone says it does, or if they say it, maybe they've not experienced real pain, or who knows anyone else's experience of anything anyway, no matter how much empathy or how many attempts at explanation. The waiting room is more pleasant than most, because this is a waiting room for only women, and there's the implication that women need that: floral print fabric on the chairs, so many magazines, pastel watercolor prints in light-wood frames, easy music. The last one of these I had done, there was a shadow in the left breast that warranted a callback and a do-over, a calcification like the one in my gall bladder: turning-to-stone twins! Two parts of my body that don't want to be human but prefer a rockiness that feels like home. So, this time, it's not only the tech, but the actual doctor in the room. "We want to be extra careful," the doctor says. Her hair is in perfect braids that hang down to her waistline, and they make a beautiful whoosh when she moves.

I should mention that we are fucking, the radiologist and me. Are you getting tired of this? Me, too. The bodies, the accumulation. Her breasts are small and taut, and pulling them between the two glass platters would likely be painful, but I can tell she's the kind of person who wouldn't say a word, because she's been trained by life to not comment on pain. Or maybe that's just something I want to assume about her. Here's another assumption: that two women together are gentle and whispering niceties in each other's ears and not hard-edged and up against the wall of the log house she built right next to the river where no one can see us in the backyard picking radishes at two A.M., naked and licking each other's faces and laughing.

When I was three, my father's extended family gathered in my aunt's house for a weekend. My aunt's 1960s car was in the driveway, and it was the baby's first birthday, and my father's parents—my grandparents—had driven up from Missouri to a Chicago suburb with presents they couldn't afford wrapped so carefully in the back seat. The first night, they ate steak grilled outside, and sat in iron chairs around an umbrella table. The baby crawled across the lawn, and my uncle took careful pictures of him because people still used film, and every picture had to count. It was summer, and they stayed up late and watched fireflies, and my aunt even collected some in a jar with the toddler and sat with him on her lap, and they clapped and screamed a happy small scream together each time the fireflies turned the glass yellow. The fire that started was a small electrical one in the wall of the house they'd moved into only a few months before, and it took its time filling the house with smoke but didn't take the house down. In the end, when their bodies were stones near windows and doors, the house was still there, intact.

This is something I think about: the way joy is temporal but can function much like a cloud over the sun. You can be in it and feel it but also know it's moving, and all my thoughts about love and life and joy and pain are sophomoric and dumb, but knowing that doesn't save me from them.

My mom is forever trying to bring me coleslaw, but I find coleslaw, its confetti of random minced vegetables in a soupy whiteness, disgusting. My mom still shows up with it in a plastic container. "You might like it, she says, try it, you never even try it," and it is true that every time she brings it, I find it a few days later untouched in the refrigerator and push the contents down the disposal and run the disposal instead of scraping it into the trash and think for ten minutes about the water treatment facility tasked with separating out all our shit from all our water. I fall down the stairs trying to greet my mother with her plastic container of coleslaw between two hands, and my leg is gashed open by the concrete. If the radiologist were there, she might take a bag out of her car, a bag of essential things she carries with her all the time, and prime and patch my leg. But she is not there. Instead, my mom, with her coleslaw, says: "stand up, get a grip, shake it off." Does she really say this? Or does she pull me over like a baby and get blood all over her own violet-colored shirt?

My sister calls me from several states away where a wildfire has taken a whole town and almost all its people. There's no need for anyone else in this scene, for any doctor to tell me the tricks they will perform to stave off impending death. Because my sister and I: we are soulmates. And we've already planned how, in our old age, we'll find an apartment with round windows like a ship, and maybe we won't even need two rooms because we'll be in a bed Willy Wonka style, right next to each other, taking us straight back to childhood with the yellow and white gingham bedspread and the jungle wallpaper with all the happy cartoon lions making us think lion-ing was easy and fun.

"It wasn't that bad," my sister says on the phone of the childhood things I've turned into haunted house chambers in my mind.

"None of it was that bad," she says. She's had the moles lasered off and the breast flattening and the hurt foot that lasts for months and reminds her that, yes, 53 is really something.

I make myself flat on my bed and cling to my sister like a life raft and keep the phone on, whatever digital madness is connecting us across a thousand miles, holding onto the past and the now and the future.

You, dear reader, perched on a rocking chair in your 1800s cap with all your narrative expectations, you will want me to change, to have changed, to have some Araby-style epiphany to save me from this 2021 life of static downward whatever. But I'm sorry. I'm the same.

Cinema

After being released from the hospital, I found a job at an old movie theater downtown. I stocked candy, cleaned bathrooms, and served local beer to people my age who always said the same things: *We haven't been to a movie in years,* and *this is so wild, we're empty nesters now.* They looked blown back and frazzled, like old babies, slightly dead but also surprised by every single thing.

Movie theaters were becoming obsolete. People preferred to lie with their phones. This theater, though, was old and architecturally beautiful with velvet folding seats and a mural of the night sky painted on the ceiling. To sit in the dark there was an exercise in pleasing sentimentality.

The last week in September, we started showing a love story set in Sicily. On the screen, vintage cars coasted down winding roads, tree branches brimmed with olives, and the beautiful chins of two people were often almost touching.

"I've never been in love like that," my manager, Leland, said after we watched the first showing through the concessions window. "I mean in love in the Italian way." His brown beard looked opaque and overfull, as if a hedgehog might be living in it.

"What is the Italian way?" I said, not because I wanted to know, but because I could tell he wanted me to ask. I wiped an inkblot of Dr. Pepper off the counter.

"You know, late-night dinners that go on and on. Wandering around on cobblestones holding hands. That kind of thing." He coughed, and it sounded treacherous.

The most in love I'd ever been was with my children, but I didn't say that to him.

Twenty minutes before the second showing, a couple with a baby asleep in a stroller bought two tickets and went to wait in the theater.

I walked through the rows of chairs to pick up discarded wrappers and cups and then stood with a trash bag at the back of the last row and watched the couple. The man moved the stroller a few inches forward and backward over and over. I couldn't imagine taking a baby to a movie. It seemed brazen and hopeful. The baby in the stroller didn't move and didn't cry.

"Stop staring," Joes said. He was the older of my two sons, and there he was on one of the velvet seats with his back to me at first, so I hadn't seen him through the dim space.

I gasped at the set of his shoulders, the line of neck visible between his t-shirt and hair. The man with the stroller turned to look at me, and his face was stern.

"They might come to you sometimes," one of the doctors at the hospital had told me before I left, but I hadn't imagined it like this.

"Seriously, Mom, it's creepy. Look away," Joes said. He was four when I last saw him, but this movie theater Joes was mid-teens, an age he never was, and with floppy skater hair he kept brushing away from his eyes and eyebrows that looked like man eyebrows instead of the boy eyebrows I could remember smoothing over with my finger while we rocked in the chair in the bedroom where I once hung an old map of San Francisco on the wall.

"You're right," I said, "I'll stop."

All I could think, though, was *it's happening again. Again, I'm losing my mind.*

One of my doctors had said, "You weren't yourself, that wasn't you." That doctor had hair like straw. He wore sneakers with suit pants. He was old, so his own mother was maybe dead, but at some point, she'd bathed him, watched him playing outside of a glass window, bought him shoes in a store. I nodded when that doctor told me in clinical terms what had happened, told me, again, it wasn't me, but I knew it *was* me. I had that in me and would carry it everywhere like a bag of teeth sewn into a pocket of my own skin.

"I know what you're thinking," Joes said, "I know you're sad. I know you're doing your whole *nostalgia* thing."

I moved around to the side of the aisle, so I could see him more fully. His shoes were both untied, and I wanted to crawl on the floor that was surely sticky with Sprite and textured with discarded kernels, so I could tie his two shoes as carefully as anyone had ever done any manual thing.

After Joes was born, I carried him down the town's main street in a cloth front carrier. We passed all the neighborhood spots: the stone wall where crocuses bloomed, the fire station, the intersection where men sat with cardboard signs that asked for food and mercy. I was sad then, but it didn't obliterate me. I had trouble with nursing, but it wasn't a moral failure. I didn't think people on the street

in front of the jewelry store or the record store were plot-
ting something with me at its center. I made dinners that
were pretty on the plate, and my husband came home in
a sweater and pants with creases and ate the dinners and
smiled at Joes and sang songs to him and read him small
stories from cloth books. We marveled at his fingers and
his hair and felt more smug than we wanted to admit about
how he did so many things before the books said he would:
smile, coo, sit up, hold himself standing.

"I should work," I said to Joes, but what I really meant was
where's Sams, where's Sams, where's my baby, and *are you—could
you possibly be—okay* and *I'm sorry, you don't know how much*
and *don't go don't go don't go.*

Joes was gone, though, before I finished the word
work. I sat in the chair where he'd been sitting to see if
it felt warm, but it was stiff and cool, so I walked back
through the door into the concessions room. I straightened
the Junior Mints, turned over the stainless popper, checked
the soda, and bit my lip hard enough that I hoped blood
would come, but it didn't. It took more than I had, apparently, to shear through skin with teeth.

Joes, Sams, those were the nicknames I'd given them
when I thought I was young and clever, when Joey and
Sammy felt too expected, when I would do things like drive
them to the farm where you could pull asparagus from the
ground and take it home to roast with garlic cloves under
the broiler. Sams in the back carrier, his arms stretching
out toward things he could never reach. Joes running ahead
on the soil that was soft and damp enough to swallow his
sneakers whole. Then, I was suffocated by sadness but also
summoned by urges. Drive to the railroad station. Board
a train with no plan. Get off thirty miles away, circle back.

Gather the two kids in the double stroller at night and stand by the road's edge. Lurk by the tracks. Gaze at the river. I wanted to think I was, then, a whole other person.

On the way to and from work each day, I biked by the house where, ten years before, I lived with a husband and two children, where now a middle-aged couple lived with their adult daughter. They'd recently affixed a wooden sign to the front door that said, "Spooky Season" and stretched the filaments of polyester webbing across the boxwoods.

The people who'd lived on the block then wouldn't recognize me anymore. In ten years, I'd lost twenty pounds, cut my hair short, let it go back to its natural, darker color, stopped wearing contacts, and gotten big cheap glasses that distracted from my face, which was gaunt now and sad.

The adult daughter who lived in my old house pulled in front and parked her red Jeep with its Life is Good tire cover that at first made me angry but then made me jealous. Cynicism had done nothing for me for decades. Smug superiority only made you feel isolated and terrible. Meanwhile, Jeep woman was riding around with the fabric doors snapped off. Probably drinking sugary coffee. Listening to loud music with a bass line that could wrap around you in a smothering warmth.

The Jeep woman went in the house's front door, and I heard laughter. I could close my eyes and picture the house: the entry with the bench seat, the dining room and its old chandelier, the half bath, the kitchen. I rode home so fast my face felt featureless and erased by the wind.

In my apartment's living room, I ate lentils from a plastic bag heated in the microwave. The room felt too warm, and I couldn't breathe. I opened all the windows.

For the whole first year in the hospital, I'd lie in bed in the plain room and think not about death, an act, but about not being, about never having been. The trial had taken weeks, and I'd been an open wound in the room, but it had been a distraction. Now, though I knew I needed to live with all of it, the thought of going away came a few times a day in the form of objects: this bed sheet, this hanger, this knife.

In the cold living room, I tried to watch a show about people who designed new clothes made from old clothes people had thrown away, but all the people had a veneer of something hovering over their real pain and anger and sadness, like the top was a clear shell, and underneath was roiling or magma.

"I feel like you could come up with a more unique description, Mom," Sams said. He sat on the other folding chair across from me. I tried to contrive my own ghost self to match him, some future me if everything had gone differently. Maybe she wore wide-legged pants. Maybe she was good at messy buns and small talk. Maybe she didn't have a wheelbarrow of sorrow to pull behind her everywhere she went.

I wanted to pick Sams up like he was a bunch of tulips wrapped in brown paper and left on a countertop, but he went fluid. He was on the chair, he was on the wall, he was playing jacks in the corner like a child of the 1950s, which of course he never ever was.

"Mom, mom, mommy," he said, but then he was a man in a suit, and I hated that, but I loved it, too, loved the forward of that for him, the progress.

I went to the bedroom and sat on the edge of the bed, and my grown-man suit son sat next to me and pointed at the pink box on the nightstand. "Mom, don't take Benadryl, it causes dementia." His feet were in shiny shoes someone might wear to an advertising agency.

"Noted," I said, but what I meant was, *I don't care anymore about that.*

After Joes was born, it hadn't been bad. After Sams came, though, I was under rocks. I was inside steel wool. I was driving and the wheel lurched to the left or the right. *I'm dying,* I said to my husband, and he laughed and said, *I know, I'm tired, too.* The birds that started coming early in the morning to say *it's spring like it or not* did me in. *I can't,* I said to my husband, and he said, *I know, it's hard, but you can.*

I asked suit-wearing Sams, "Where's Joes?" though I felt sure if I asked anything sad, he'd disappear. "Are you and Joes together sometimes?" I asked because I wanted that so much.

Sams swung his long legs over the side of the bed. He didn't answer. Instead, he said, "Don't fall asleep with a cough drop in your mouth. Don't drink too much water, and yes there is such a thing. Avoid candles altogether."

Why are you thinking of danger, I almost asked, but didn't.

He said, "Ha, Mom, that's funny," and it was a knife, though he hadn't meant it as one.

"I miss you, Sams," I said, "I miss you," and then the room filled with so many versions of him. They flickered the way a glitching computer screen would, and then they were gone.

In the morning, the trees outside the open window, cone-shaped pines in huddles, pulsed with chickadees. I walked out the back door and sat in the wet grass, so the sound was all around, and it made me feel miniaturized and inside another human body, traveling through an artery in a fast slide down toward the pump pumping of a human heart.

◆

For the last of September and all the days of October, it was like this. Joes in the bathtub. Sams hiding behind the conifer in the backyard. Joes at a stoplight by the liquor store. Sams at the table in the kitchen. Joes curled up in the storage cabinet at work. Sams hanging onto the Life is Good tire cover on the back of the woman's Jeep while she pulled quickly away.

I didn't have anyone to ask about it, so when someone selling solar panels called, I said, "This isn't really my house," and then without pausing, "I'm seeing things."

The solar panel salesman said, "That happens to me sometimes, too."

I said, "Really? I don't even know if they're real, like actual ghosts, or if I'm imagining them to help me somehow."

The salesman said, "That's a conundrum. But does it matter why it's happening?" I heard him take a drink of something through a straw.

"True," I said, and then "I guess not," and then, "What do you do anyway, I mean when you see things?"

The man said, "I say, 'that's not really there' over and over until whatever it was is gone."

"I'll try it," I told him, but I knew I wouldn't.

The man said, "I wish you the best of luck," like I was on a ship, and he was on the shore, and he was watching the ship back away toward the skyline.

After the call, I rode down the sidewalk of the busy street that led away from the neighborhood where I was living and toward the older neighborhoods and downtown. In the field beside me, one of the few empty fields remaining in the town where people had turned other once-empty fields into apartment complexes and gyms and drive-thru coffee places, I saw a coyote, ragged, distressed, loping. None of the people in the cars looked out their windows, so maybe it wasn't real. A *coyote!* I wanted to whisper in all their ears, but I kept moving my legs, down the hill, up the hill, to Iowa Street until Joes was there on one of those wooden bikes with no pedals, but he was flying. His feet splayed out to the sides like wings.

"I saw it, Mom," he said. "The coyote! You wanted someone to see it, and I saw it!" He was five or six or seven, what I imagined would be the sweetest age.

"Later, let's make popcorn balls," I said in the wind. "Let's sit under the red blanket and watch that movie about the big dog or the show about the nice dinosaurs."

Joes said, "It's okay, Mommy. You know we aren't mad."

On Halloween, my manager, Leland, sliced his hand on the metal trash can while taking out the recycling and had to be driven by a friend to the emergency room for stitches. The projectionist said, "I hate this fucking holiday," when he showed up, and then he remained in his booth. I left Leland's oval of blood on the linoleum and handled concessions for three back-to-back screenings of the Italian love movie.

Children who were giraffes or cats or garbage cans or houses made of cardboard boxes or TV show characters I didn't recognize or small versions of something their parents were also dressed as came into the open double doors to ask for candy. Leland had left drywall buckets full of the cheap kind of candy you get in bulk. Sixlets. Dumdums. Smarties. The kids dropped the candy into pillowcases or Target bags or plastic pumpkins while their parents told them: "Say thank you! Say Happy Halloween! Say trick or treat!"

I'd trick-or-treated with Joes but not with Sams, and I could call to mind Joes as a baby pumpkin. Joes as Yoda with green face makeup he kept smearing off with his finger. Joes as...a pirate? A dinosaur? I wanted to but couldn't remember the other one.

In the middle of the third screening, when the sky had gone from both lavender and orange at the tree line to navy, when the kids coming in were eleven and twelve and not four and five, I dumped the remaining bucket of candy out on the table by the door and told everyone who came in to take a few.

I looked for Sams and Joes in the groups, but they didn't come. Maybe wanting it made it not happen. Maybe expecting it was the problem.

The credits rolled inside the theater, and the people from the final showing walked out into the night in clumps and pairs. The kids were all gone, the younger ones asleep, fingers twitching with sugar, the older ones comparing candy in dens and living rooms.

A man came in dressed like a zombie. His face was intricately made up to look carved away. It was both admirable and ridiculous, the trouble that had been taken to make him look post-dead.

"We're closed," I told him, "Or closing."

"What if I said I had a gun, and I need money?" he said.

I couldn't tell if he was serious, but I saw in him the brittle bad part I knew I had, too, and I was immediately unafraid. "Okay, shoot me," I said. I wanted the worst thing or for, finally, something to be worse than the worst thing, which had already happened.

He started laughing, then laughed so hard he had to sit in the chair by the table with the candy. "Really, I'm just drunk. I don't have a gun." He pulled his knees up to his chest like a child. "I do have a knife," he said, but when he pulled it out, I saw it as the kind of knife that a restaurant server brings with a bread plate. "I'm pathetic," he said and stood up.

The projectionist waved goodnight and walked out the front door.

"Time to close," I said to the man, walked to the back, and turned off all the lights.

"Can I come with you?" the man asked when I got back to the concessions area with my bike.

It had been years since I'd really talked to a man not a doctor or not for work. At the end of the time at the hospital, I tried calling my husband, even though I knew there was no way to apologize. He said, "I can't," and hung up, and I understood completely.

"I was at a bar, but I don't want to go back, and there's no way I'm going home."

"I have my bike," I said and looked down at it. I didn't need details about why home was not a place he could go. I recognized the shape of his desperation.

"Can I walk your bike, and then we can walk together?"

I'd only been out for a few months, and I'd denied myself everything during that time, and that was the plan for the future, too. No decent food. No sugar. No alcohol. No car. No place to live that I liked. No different kind of job. No companionship.

"I don't know you at all," I said. "You don't know me." I locked the theater's doors. Candy wrappers patterned the sidewalk, and a whole plastic arm dropped from a costume sat next to a planter full of yellow mums.

"Okay, I'm John. Drunk John, you can call me, but that will pass, and I'll just be John. I'm divorced. I was a terrible husband. I work in a greeting card factory. I live in a studio. I'm not a murderer. I'm not dangerous, I mean. What else? I like Tom Waits too much." He rolled the sleeves of his white shirt up, and there was a picture of Tom Waits' face tattooed on his forearm. "That was a mistake," he said, "But I was young."

It would be nice if people's mistakes rolled in front of them on some kind of digital banner you could preview and decide whether talking to them was worth it. I'd never have to tell anyone what I did, say it aloud, worry. They could read my banner and walk away quickly or even run.

"I'm not fun to be around," I said to the man.

"Oh, who cares? Fun is dumb," he said.

We walked past the empty public pool with its tube slides. We walked into the neighborhood where I once carried Joes in one arm and a plastic car he refused to ride in the other arm for eight blocks from the park to home.

The man and I walked past the house with the towers of stones in the side yard. We walked past the place where crows in spring had argued at the bird feeder.

"I'm not drunk anymore," John said. He picked up a Mardi Gras necklace someone had dropped and wrapped it around his wrist.

When we reached my old house, I saw my old next-door neighbors on their front porch carrying a small table and candy bowl back into their house. They were old now and fragile. They'd raised their own kids in their house, and I hated to think of the memories they faced each day when doing the most mundane things, the way parenting could be a slow unfurling of a long ribbon. The kids on the other end kept going until they were out of sight, and they could still see the ribbon and sometimes feel a tug, but the kids were gone.

"Do you want to keep walking?" the man asked me.

The red Jeep woman came out onto the porch of my old house and said, "Hey, why don't you come in? I see you every day. You should come in. We're having a party."

The woman seemed drunk. Maybe almost everyone over a certain age was drunk on Halloween, but I wasn't. I didn't want to go in, but suddenly that's what we were doing. The man, John, the woman, the woman's parents, a bunch of other people I didn't recognize in my old house where music played, and a head-sized plastic spider hung from the light fixture. All the rooms had been painted jewel tones: eggplant and ruby and teal, even though they'd been the palest pink when I lived there.

The Jeep woman handed me a drink. I hadn't had alcohol in ten years, but the woman said, "Drink," and I did. The woman said, "Yes!" and pounded her hand on the table, where my square-edged Ikea table had been, with Sams' highchair and Joes' booster.

The woman started talking to the man about a water park being built by the river, and I went upstairs and sat in the room that was now an office but before had belonged to Joes, where he'd once laughed as he pulled himself to standing in the crib, where he'd sat on the braided rug playing with finger-sized pieces of driftwood, watching birds on the tree branch outside the east-facing window.

With a black Sharpie, I drew a thick line on the floor around where Joes' crib and then toddler bed had once been. I drew a square on the wood where the rocking chair once was and where I'd rocked both children and where I'd been bad and good and all the things a person could be. I wouldn't be able to ride by the house again after this. It was okay, though. The worst punishment, anyway, was to keep being flung into a new day with all that space for remembering.

I walked downstairs and into the backyard, and all I wanted was for Joes and Sams to appear. The night sky was filmy and strange. The muffled music coming from inside made me feel underwater. I tried to trick myself into thinking Joes was climbing a tree, or Sams was emerging from the light flickering by the shed where we stored an old push mower, but they were nowhere.

The man came outside and said, "There you are." He'd washed his face completely clean, and I could see it was a nice face. I could imagine eating a meal across from it, but I couldn't see how to tell another face what it was that I'd done.

"Let's go," the man said. He pulled on my jacket sleeve, grabbed my bike from where it was leaning at the side of the house, and I followed him away from the house and up the street.

We walked toward campus to the place with the pond encircled by cattails. What was I going to do? Bring this man back to a nearly empty apartment, make him microwave popcorn, watch bad TV, let him sit and wonder while I looked into an empty room for the ghosts or visions of my dead children? Also, it was preposterous, given everything, to even think of the possibility of sex.

Geese bedded in the cattails made noises in their sleep. A turtle rested on one of the rock slabs that made a path across the water. The man put his foot close to the turtle, but the turtle didn't slide off the rock and into the water. "It's dead, poor guy," he said and covered it with dry leaves. We sat on the grass. A curtain of clouds covered the moon and the stars.

I used to listen to a Joni Mitchell song over and over with Joes when he couldn't sleep. He'd look right at me when Joni said, "the night is a starry dome," and the moonlight through the window made Joes' face glow, and his open eyes held everything. I knew I would never have anything like that again, but maybe having had it was enough.

"It's getting too cold," the man said, so we walked all the blocks back to the theater. I avoided the street with my old house and instead walked through the alleys where I was somehow not shattered when the clouds parted to show the moon: a white ball, a shining place faraway, a chasm. The man held onto my hand, and I let him.

In the alley behind the theater, a transformer box buzzed. We could see our breath. I unlocked the back door.

"We left my bike at the lake," I said when I realized it. The metal skeleton of it leaned against the willow tree by the pond where my ex-husband and I had strung hammocks on some weekend days. Maybe Joes or Sams would jump on it and ride it over water or up the hills where in summer dandelions made a yellow sea.

"We'll get it. It'll be there," the man said.

The man followed me up to the projection booth, and we figured out how to start the Italian love movie. I turned the volume as high as it could go, so high that the man and I had to put our hands over our ears when we made our way down to the theater, when we lay on the stage immediately in front of the screen while the two faces of the Italian actors came together, while they sat on a boat and were not made sick by the waves.

"I like when noise is so loud you can't think," the man said.

"Wait, what? What did you say?" I said because at first it was just word jumble, but then it made sense. "Yes," I said. "Same."

The man hung onto my forearm. When the Italian actors kissed for what felt like minutes, we laughed and laughed, until we were coughing and breathless, because love was, really, as preposterous as anything.

Sad Grownups

Childhood geniuses level out. They become sad grownups. At least that's what had happened to Odon and his friend Mac.

They'd met in fifth grade, where, during the first week of school, one of their classroom hamsters killed his cage-mate, and they'd all stood around the garden at the edge of the playground while their teacher dug with a spoon in the dirt and placed a stapler box of hamster remains in a hole in the ground. "I don't give a shit about dead hamsters," Mac had said to Odon at the back of the pack of children. "Hamster, singular, not hamsters, plural," Odon said back to Mac. "Touché," Mac said, except he pronounced it incorrectly and without the accent in the way of someone who had read a lot but not actually talked to many people, but it was enough for Odon to instantly recognize Mac as one of his own.

From then, they were always together. Even though Odon was always a head taller and gangly as fuck, and Mac looked like a child Rachel Maddow and maybe believed at first that he needed Odon as some kind of shield or protection. They often dressed as twins, not to be clever but for the utility of it, in Steve Jobs-esque uniforms of black jeans and black hoodies. They gathered detritus from Odon's garage and designed an elaborate conveyer machine that did nothing more than ferry candy to them from Odon's kitchen. They wrote sci-fi novels that featured detached and electrified human arms taking over a city. They made food-based bets before timing each other solving multi-page math problems. They had promise. They had potential. Everyone said so.

But now, at nineteen and having dropped out after a semester of college at the un-brag-worthy university in the town where they'd grown up, Mac and Odon spent evenings in Odon's mom's attic doing a few things: smoking weed, playing a modified two-person version of Settlers of Catan, and eating Takis. And it was in this haze that was one part giving up and two parts delayed-adolescent agitation, they came up with a plan.

Wendy Huang worked at a bagel place on the sad strip that had once been a highway through their town but now, thanks to a bypass, wasn't even that. Wendy was, according to Odon, perfect, but denied and resisted her own perfection, and this made her even more so. She was putting herself through college and turning over her small bagel-associated paychecks to her mom, and even though she'd gotten a full ride to better places out of state, she'd stayed in town to go to the local university because she was the oldest girl in a family of four with a single mother who did alterations at a windowless place near the bagel shop where formal and prom seasons were a fucking nightmare with the sorority girls and their thousand-dollar dresses that had to be shorter or show more side boob, and, yes, they needed that in twenty-four hours.

It was not an overstatement to say Odon was obsessed with Wendy. He'd scoffed at romance and love for most of his life. His mother was long divorced, and she'd never dated after his dad left. She spent most nights sitting in their living room with her sister who lived down the street, drinking boxed wine, listening to music, and mocking people. And because it was easier to not feel, but also to be her disciple, he'd adopted the same attitude. People in his high school hallways who practically fucked against lockers were weak and all urge and no superego, and he and Mac, who, by this point, habitually followed along with Odon, would do dramatic eye rolls when passing these displays. It was easy to keep it like that, to maintain that dynamic and emotional distance, for ninth, and tenth, and eleventh grades when he and Mac sailed through Calc II early and each submitted full-length novels to small presses and led a robotics team to a national victory and were all-state in Debate. Until Wendy Huang.

This is a love story. Or really, maybe it's a story of wanting but not understanding love, and maybe that's the saddest love story of all.

Odon had almost never spoken to Wendy, aside from a hello or a nod in Calc or Debate. But for several years, he'd watched her. He knew if he admitted this to anyone but Mac, it would sound predatory. Still, he knew the following: Wendy lived with her mother and sisters in a duplex. Once after a snowstorm, he'd seen Wendy standing in the yard looking at her phone while one of her younger sisters stuffed another sister into a plastic storage container and pushed her on a track they'd made through the snow. Wendy preferred Linear Algebra to Calc. She liked Indian food. Her birthday was May 11. She drove an older-model Prius to drop her mother at work before backtracking to park on campus where she sometimes sat in her car, sometimes with her head on the steering wheel. In high school, she had been quiet, but he'd once seen her jump on the back of a girl she sometimes walked with, and the girl started running with Wendy piggy-backing, and they were both laughing so hard it made Odon think for a second before he blotted it out as unnecessary and damaging that he didn't know Wendy at all.

Through all of the pre-spring weeks when there was that breath-holding and chill that came before the daffodils fully opened and the forsythias shot yellow across their spines, Odon developed a plan: to rob the bagel shop on a Thursday in late March and then drop the cash mid-day when no one was at Wendy's house because he assumed she and her sisters could really use the money. He imagined them opening such an envelope by their front door and the celebratory looks on their faces and the way they might cast out toward the sidewalk in wonder to see if anyone was watching or if they could take this envelope inside and call it their own. Or at least the sisters would, not Wendy, who would pull it away and save it for their mother because, Odon knew, she was selfless in the way of a Mother Teresa or a Gandhi.

And so those were the exact masks Odon and Mac ordered because 1) Odon decided Wendy would be pleased with the choices and 2) Mac agreed there would be an edge of unexpected hilarity for Mother Teresa and Gandhi to rob a bagel shop on Thursday mid-day after their busy two-for-one special when everyone seemed to come in inexplicably with cash, even though cash was, elsewhere, nearly obsolete.

Some friendships are the melding of two people with similar levels of power, and some friendships are comprised of leader and acolyte, and Odon and Mac's friendship had always been the latter. As such, Odon orchestrated the plan, and he and Mac mapped out and practiced the steps start to finish, many nights in a row in Odon's attic while they heard squirrels chewing and making inroads into the eaves and soffits that ran along both sides of the attic room. If he stepped back from the plan, Odon would see it made no sense at all, but he was too deep in to do anything more than believe in it fully, and Mac, devoted sideman, would never voice any concerns even if he had them, which Odon was sure he probably did.

When Mac left at night, Odon, alone with the squirrel noises and the branches tapping at the skylights with the wind, sometimes put his hands over his ears and cried for reasons he wouldn't have been able to articulate, not for a million dollars, not even gun to head.

The bagel place where Wendy worked was in the small shopping area that someone in the 1970s planned to look like a Swiss village, and no one since had the time or money or motivation to redesign. It was white stucco and dark brown beams with shop letters in scrolled ironwork for signs that had been around forever and incongruous lighted plastic for those that had not.

Mac and Odon sat in the car in the parking lot for a solid thirty minutes, and no one reacted to them in any way. Not the woman tugging a toddler with one hand while holding a bag of dog food half her size with the other. Not the man vaping in his car before setting out for the hardware store. And definitely not the couple in puffy jackets fighting in front of the gaming place.

It probably goes without saying, but off-the-charts abstract reasoning scores did not prepare one for the logistics of crime. They might, however, give one the misplaced confidence required to think crime was 100% possible.

At some point in their planning, Odon had decided it would be better for Mac to be the only one in a mask, for Mac to come in the bagel shop while Odon was positioned at a table by the register and for Odon to step in to protect Wendy, to chase Mac away, to save her from harm. Every single thing Odon's mother had taught him should have forewarned him that Wendy didn't need saving and that to think so was an insult, and he really knew this on some level, but he still wanted so badly to do it anyway.

Odon knew from the way Mac was sitting, though, from the way he was waiting, and breathing faster than normal and wouldn't look right at Odon, that Mac didn't want to do any of this. Odon knew he should have absolved Mac, driven him home, let him sit in this bedroom with the chalkboard wall full of equations and catch his breath. That would have been the right thing, he knew that, but he didn't do it, even though he could see, sitting in the parking lot, there was no logic to robbing the place where Wendy worked to give Wendy the money. Odon had felt in the planning like there was a beautiful cleanness to it, but in the minutes before the execution of the plan, he knew he'd been horribly wrong. He knew Mac had known this the whole time, too, and Odon wondered if it was the best or worst friend thing ever for him not to have said anything.

Odon got out of the car first. He knew from past trips to the shop that the door had a bell in the shape of a dolphin that rang when the door opened and closed. A ringing dolphin made little sense to him, but he tried not to think about it as he walked to the register to order an everything bagel and coffee to pour into the metal mug he's somehow remembered to bring from home, all from Wendy Huang who gave him a familiar, "Oh, hey," while ringing him up and counting out coins in his hand. It was the time of day when old men drank endless coffee alone at tables and read sections of the paper that they traded with each other.

Odon settled in with the classifieds, and it was hard to believe, with Facebook Marketplace and Craigslist, that people still posted ads in a newspaper that almost no one but the aging and aged read, but he leaned in close as if reading something very important to wait the pre-planned five minutes for Mac to enter.

"Which mask should I wear? Teresa or Gandhi?" Mac had asked Odon in the car. "Surprise me," Odon had said, and he is actually surprised when Mac walks in wearing Teresa because Mac was vehemently anti-Catholic and often went on quiet tirades about organized Christian religions, but Odon assumed that was sort of the point, that in this mask, Mac was even less recognizably himself.

When Mac walked to the register, Odon watched but tried not to watch too hard. He didn't want to give anything away, but he got transfixed by the hair on the back of Mac's neck below his hairline but above his shirt. It was a dark fur, and he wondered why no one, no barber, not his mother, had told Mac to shave it, and, even more so, he wondered why after all this time together he had never noticed it.

Things happened quickly. Mac said something about needing all the money. Mac had his hands in his pockets, and anyone who has watched any crime show knows that this would suggest a mystery weapon that was likely nothing but a screwdriver or a carrot or a fist but could be something still. Odon could only see Wendy's face, and it was blank but also undaunted, like she had been expecting this, like nothing could surprise her.

She opened the register and started to gather bills. For a beat too long, Odon was held by her expression, and he realized right then that he never had a chance with her. He realized the idea of a person is thin and paper and nothing up against the actual person.

He was supposed to get up to intervene very soon; it was what he and Mac practiced so many times. But he didn't do it. He looked at Wendy's face, and it was only an extra second, but in that second, one of the old men got up and pulled a gun out of who knows what crazy kangaroo pouch under his sports-team nylon jacket and, without even a pause, shot Mac. Then Mac was on the floor, and his Mother Teresa mask was askew so that Odon, who sank down low over Mac's face, saw half Mother Teresa and half Mac in a way that was so almost existentially confusing, Odon passed out.

When he woke, there were paramedics, and the Mother Teresa mask was on the floor face up, as if Mother Teresa herself had clawed up from underground, and only her face had broken through but the rest of her was surely coming soon. Mac was in a plastic oxygen mask. Mac was on a stretcher. Mac was being carried out the door. Wendy? She was nowhere. The old man with the gun was talking to police, and Odon heard one of them saying, "You did

what you had to do." This angered Odon more than anything because there was almost no scenario in which an old
man in a bagel shop needed to shoot a nineteen-year-old
demanding singles in a Midwestern strip mall.

In a better version of this story, Odon would chase Mac
out, and Wendy would be cheering for him. Or he'd get
into a math-off with a still-masked Mac, and he'd out-
math him, and then Mac would run out unharmed, and
Odon and Wendy would split a sesame bagel and laugh
together about the charming oddity of the whole thing,
and he'd brush sesame seeds off her chin, and he'd see her
startle and smile at the fun electricity of it all. He'd meet
her sisters, and they'd love him immediately. His mother
would make them cookies and send them on a road trip
without piling on any guilt about his leaving her there in
the house alone.

What happens instead is this: Mac spends three weeks
in the hospital. Odon gets one text from Mac's number
that says, "It's best for you not to visit." He knows from the
word choice and punctuation that it is not actually Mac,
and amazingly after all their years, that is that.

Even though they'd planned it together, the spin is somehow that it's all Odon's fault, and Odon knows this is probably very accurate.

Odon goes to his phone a thousand times to text Mac
but doesn't. He does a few sad drive-bys around Wendy's
block and then, as penance, forbids himself from doing
so ever again. He listens to all his mom's vinyl on a small
portable record player in the attic, so it sounds scratchier
than it should and awful, but he thinks he deserves it. He
spends nine weeks working through much of the Criterion

Collection on Hulu. He builds nothing. He writes nothing. His mom and his aunt call up from the landing in the evenings. They blast "September" and beg him to come down, but he won't.

It's a Saturday in June when he and his mother are standing in the kitchen eating ramen for breakfast and his mother tells him she ran into Mac's mother at the co-op, that Mac has only a slight limp, that Mac's parents have set him up in a studio apartment near MIT where he'd deferred admission the previous fall and was scheduled to start classes in a few months.

Odon blinks too many times at his mother. He can't believe that for a little over a full year, Mac had been holding in the fact of this college admission, the school that had been their first choice but that had rejected Odon. Mac had claimed on the day they'd found out that he'd been rejected, too. They'd both walked to the burrito place after finding out at their separate houses, bought what they called "rejection burritos" and then "Fuck MIT burritos," and the whole time, the whole night, as they'd walked all around town bemoaning the ugly world of college admissions, Mac had been sitting on his acceptance and not saying a thing.

Now, per Odon's mom, Mac is spending the summer working in a bookshop a couple of T stops from MIT, a store known for its extensive collection of vintage science fiction.

"I've actually been there," she says. The hot water kettle bubbles, and she pours water into a mug. "There's a lot of signed first edition stuff there, you'd love it," she says, and this is her way of saying he should go there and see it for himself, or at least that he should do something that isn't this kitchen, this attic, this house, this town.

He puts down his bowl of ramen and walks out the back door into the yard where everything is green: lily stems, grass that shouldn't grow where they live, the leaves of the maple tree he and Mac had climbed to loft objects into the neighbor's yard. He hadn't really known Wendy, and he hadn't really known Mac, or he'd only known as much of Mac as Mac had let him or as much as he, Odon, wanted to see, and maybe that was how knowing people would go.

Would it be good to say, several months later, in September, when the windows of the attic are open, and he has unplugged the TV for good and painted the room white, and he can hear the tips of tree branches tapping up against the house in a gentle and not foreboding way, that he's moved on from Wendy? Okay, for the most part, he has. But he's still in his mother's attic, alone.

He looks out the attic window and sees in the streak of the outdoor light the spot in the eaves that extends out from the house to make a delicate wooden pocket where the squirrels have built a large nest out of leaves and sticks and the stuffing from various deck pillows they've stolen and torn apart. He doesn't want to be sad or angry or stuck. He stuffs his pockets with all his accumulated ones and fives and twenties, packs his duffel, looks online for bus ticket prices, puts on his Gandhi mask, heads down the stairs, past the chaos of his mom and aunt dancing, and walks out into the night.

More Fun in the New World

My mother is only fifty when my father dies by suicide in a mental health facility devoted solely to preventing such an outcome. Belts had been confiscated at check-in. His portable radio was taken apart with a screwdriver by a delicate-handed orderly searching its innards for blades and pills. One of a troupe of nurses tipped a head in his room every ten minutes. *Suicide watch* it was called, a spectator sport. Somehow, they'd missed a robe sash in the secret lining of his vintage suitcase, a case his own father had taken on a ship across the Atlantic in 1910, a secret lining where his father had hidden Hungarian coins, a pocket watch, and a photo of his own mother.

People arrive with food after the funeral. Most of the food is ugly in rectangular vats and designed for quick consumption or freezing, as if we are feed cattle, which would have disgusted my father who had organized orange slices in pretty fans on the plates of my childhood.

My mother sits far back on the green velvet couch wearing a necklace my father bought for her when they first met.

Its beads are the size of animal eggs, and it looks like the solar system if a giant strung it on wire to carry around with him.

"We found it at an art fair in a town north of San Francisco," I hear her saying over and over to this person and then that person. Her hands hold onto the beads as if she is in water, sinking, and they might keep her afloat.

I have two jobs this summer in between my first and second years of college (restaurant and retail). I stop showing up to both. There is then a series of weeks when I lie with my mother in the back yard on a down blanket, both of us face down and in defiance of the mosquitoes that machete our legs with blood and bites. I don't think we eat, but probably we do. Actually, yes, we eat. By the end of this series of weeks, the lawn around the blanket is covered with food waste: fruit rinds, cellophane in colors, an overturned, empty container of rainbow sherbet.

I'm not sure if it's weekday or weekend when we both leave in the car without plan or destination. I'm not even sure if we close or lock the doors.

"Take it all," my mother says from the driver's seat, making a sweeping motion with one hand in the direction of the house.

It's July, and sprinklers up and down the block tick in the early morning. The house is near the city's art gallery where people line up for family photos on the grounds of the sculpture garden.

"Art! Seriously? Art?" my mother scoffs as we head west and out of the Midwestern city of my childhood.

We drive until we can't drive anymore, and there are several things I could say about it:

1. The highway from Kansas City is one long west-going line past old churches in farm fields and cows that sometimes stand shoulder-high and side-by-side in oval ponds and birds that dip down and almost touch the windshield at sixty-five miles an hour but then manage to dart away at the right moment.

2. We can listen to David Bowie's "Five Years" on cassette over and over (stop, rewind, stop, play, stop, rewind, repeat), that part where things go from measured to operatic more times than you might think, and it doesn't get old.

3. It's probably best not to stand arm in arm with my mother under an irrigation sprinkler on someone else's property, but the relentlessness of water does make me feel like I've peeled my skin back in a way that is both painful and necessary.

4. Much of the road from Durango, Colorado to Farmington, New Mexico is un-simple with switchbacks. I read true crime books aloud to my mother while she takes a turn too quickly, and yells "Sheer drop-off to the right," and starts laughing hysterically. Another turn and then "Sheer drop-off to the left!" She thinks it's funny, and though I do not, I give it to her. In the book I read aloud, Diane Downs, Oregon mother of three, has pulled her car outside the entrance to her small town's emergency room and won't stop with the horn. All three of her children have been shot, and it's clear, though not stated yet in the book, that she is the one to have shot them. "See?" my mother says as she winds around another turn, and the tops of pines cut into clouds. "See? Things could be worse." But then she is crying, and so am I.

5. It will become clear in some motel in Grand Junction or Wendover that my packing was haphazard. My mother's

opened suitcase holds linen pants and a few of my father's commemorative 10k t-shirts. Mine has two rain jackets and no socks.

6. It's best not to realize that the series of postcards my father sent from his last inpatient facility have been left behind in some truck stop bathroom in Abilene or Limon or Idaho Springs, those cards each penned with one sentence: "I'm friends with a morbidly obese man named Aaron who knits" and "I'm beginning to like the forced Tai Chi" and "All the food here seems to be cantaloupe" and "None of this is your fault."

We end up in Las Vegas. This is before the food revolution, when there are mainly buffets and no famous chefs, and the hotel's front door is a rectangle carved out of a sculptural stucco lion. We walk into the lion's neck.

"Who thought of this? Really, who?" my mother asks in a voice too loud, but it's Vegas so it doesn't matter. I can remember my father *shh*-ing my mother in several hotel lobbies during childhood vacations, but I also remember them standing close and forgetting I was in the room.

My mother is in a red "Hospital Hill 10K" t-shirt and white linen pants. I'm in one of the raincoats snapped closed over a yellow bra, and it's 109 degrees outside but crisp inside with what I imagine is a building-sized air conditioner blasting the whole place, and it's all dizzy-making lights and smoke and women in sequined bikinis with trays of drinks adorning each palm. Living beyond a parent who has chosen not to is a lot like walking after someone has cut off your feet.

First thing, we buy shirts and shorts and swimming suits in one of many gift shops and go—terrycloth and neon—to the pool on the twenty-fifth floor where most of the people sitting in lounge chairs around the water are the old and the drinking.

I jump in and lie on the blue-painted bottom of the pool until I feel like my lungs will explode or implode. When I come up, an older man with the kind of thick and perfect white hair of the patriarch in a soap opera is sitting in the chair next to my mother, and next to him is a boy who is maybe younger than I am but probably my age. The boy's hair is over his eyes, he wears mailman shorts and old Vans, and he's reading *The Mysteries of Pittsburgh,* like everyone else age eighteen to twenty-two that summer.

"Hey," he says, and I say "hey" back, and then he returns to his book, and I spread out on the chair and cover my face with a towel and for many minutes listen to my mother talk to the man while she pretends to be someone else. She's from New York, she tells him. In truth, she was born in Pittsburgh and has lived most of her life in Kansas City. She's driving me to Stanford, she tells him. The reality is that I go to an unimpressive state school near the house where I grew up. "Big family, yes," she tells him. She has no siblings. "Owned a restaurant in Soho before selling it recently," she tells him. She can barely cook. My father made multi-course meals, while she smoked on the brick patio or played solitaire while listening to NPR at the kitchen table.

Finally, I fall asleep under the white tent of the towel and have the same dream about my father that I've been having every night. I hate dreams, and I'd rather not have them, ever, because of the trick and mindfuck of them, because of the there and not there of them. In this dream, my father is in a massive body of water. I'm on the shore, and my father is trying to save his younger brother from drowning on a hot day on a small Kansas lake in 1955, the brother who went on to overdose intentionally in a hotel room in New Orleans a year after their other brother's car was hit by a train. It was a family striated with tragedy and grief, and in the dream my mother is always this giant floating face behind my shoulder saying, "Of course," and then, "We all knew it was coming," and she's looking at my father as he is putting his own head under water, and again she says, "We all knew," and in real life, we all did.

When I wake up, my mother and the man are gone. The boy is asleep in the chair next to me with *The Mysteries of Pittsburgh* on his stomach rising and falling with his breath. The sky is still bright, but the outdoor lights have come on. Everything is filmy and disorienting.

I elbow the boy.

"Oh, hey," he says. He shakes his bangs to the side in a way I can tell he knows looks good. His legs have burned, and his shin bones are pink and shiny. I notice he has a ribbon of scars all the way up one leg, and I wonder: plate glass window, car accident, unshakeable childhood infection?

"I think your mom went to the party with my grandfather," he says. "She told me to tell you." I try to do the age math that makes my mother and his grandfather a possible pairing but then give up. I don't let myself wonder where any of this is going: my mom and this grandfather, the hotel party. Instead, I force myself to run through a series of dropping-off-my-father images the way you might step down on a sprained ankle to see if it's better when you know it's not. My father at the door to a hospital in Omaha, at a holistic health center in Iowa City, a mountain retreat with hot springs in northern Colorado, the ER in Kansas City, always with a look on his face like a child's.

When the boy gets up, I pull on the yellow terrycloth shorts and the shirt from the gift shop and follow him to a suite on the floor below the penthouse where, in the middle of a crowded room, my mother and the grandfather are sitting on a sectional passing a bottle of tequila between them.

"Drink?" the boy asks and thrusts a shot glass in my direction. I drink it and then take another. My mother and the grandfather walk toward one of the suite's bedrooms and close the door. My entire body is sunburned, and it hurts to lean back against the wall, but I do so to steady myself. The boy pushes his hips into mine and starts kissing me while moving me in the direction of the other open bedroom.

All the sex I've had has been strategically obliterating. It's never delicate, and it's almost never about feeling. This is no different. I am up against a beige wall next to a water-color of a slot machine—a medium that doesn't quite fit the subject matter—and my shorts and swimming suit are around my ankles. The only real difference between this and the other obliterative sex in my past is that I'm fairly sure my mother is doing the same thing in the hotel bedroom adjacent to this one, and, even if it weren't happening so close to the day of my father's death, that's something I'd prefer not to imagine.

When we finish and I know my back and elbows are scraped to possibly bleeding and we are both quiet enough to hear the air conditioner cycle on, I pull my clothes up and walk out of the bedroom, out of the suite, down in the elevator where a woman in a teal cocktail dress applies mascara, past the front desk where a troupe of realtors is checking in for a convention, out of the lion entrance, and onto the street.

In the gift store clothes, I look like a runaway or a tourist, either of which could really fit. It's dark but still ninety degrees, and every group is a bachelor party. I am suddenly nothing but angry at my parents, those giant loping children, all need and ineptitude and no restraint.

Everywhere I look signs glow words: Silver City, Circus Circus, Enter the Night. If I were a different kind of person, I'd get onto a waiting bus to see where it would take me, but the fact is, I'll end up in my mother's car the next morning driving west and hearing the details of her night that I will not want to hear.

When I round the corner, a man standing in front of a parking lot next to a diner is getting punched repeatedly by another man. Both of them wear uniform shirts, and the man getting hit takes it, over and over, and keeps standing. He doesn't punch back even once. There's no circle of cheering people around them yelling "Fight, fight, fight" like in a movie. Instead, everyone keeps walking past them, quickly, as if it isn't happening.

For some reason I don't understand then and probably won't later, I run to their circle of motion and put myself between them, so close that I can see the bruising starting around the one man's eyes and the way he licks a drop of blood from the corner of his mouth.

"Hit me!" I yell to the one man. "Please."

At least I think I say it. At least I think I remember the punch landing and splitting the skin of my cheek. At least I think I remember driving all the way to the Pacific with my mother the next day with the windows mainly down and the music loud and a scab blooming across my face. At least I think I remember cupping salt water and dipping my face into it so I could feel the sting. But maybe I didn't. Maybe I keep walking. Maybe I say nothing to no one. Maybe I get on a bus and sleep until Seattle. Who knows? None of this is familiar. None of this is anything like the world I have known.

The Game

"Truth or dare," Sage says. Two hours into dinner with the new neighbors, she's run out of better things to say. Monty, her husband, shrugs, seems game, but Sage is sure she sees the neighbors smirk when they look at each other. The neighbors, Anna and Haru, are smart people, academics, who, unlike Sage and Monty, probably never played truth or dare when they were teenagers. Now they are all almost forty, an age no one young ever thinks they will be.

"Truth," Anna says. She's smoking one of Sage's cigarettes, and she keeps repositioning the cigarette and staring at it. Anna and Haru moved into Sage and Monty's rental house down the hill a few months ago.

Though Sage has said "we should all get together" to Anna several times in passing, this is the first time they've done it. The four of them around Sage's farm table on the stone terrace by the pool. They'd finished dinner: chickens from someone's flock down the road—killed, drained of blood, plucked, and roasted by Monty. Fresh bread with butter churned nearby. Hunks of watermelon coated in lime and sea salt. A pea and mint salad Sage bought in town and transferred to a wooden bowl. Earl Grey ice cream topped with pistachio brittle and whipped cream, those little add-ons the only things Sage made.

Now it's fully dark. They've pushed their chairs back from the table, and they are drinking. Live oaks wind a skeletal circle around the patio. Coyotes howl nearby, likely stalking some smaller animal around the dark trunks of the pomegranate trees Sage had planted when her boys were little and delighted by the refracting jewels inside a cracked-open piece of fruit.

"Okay then, truth," Sage says. She knows her voice is too loud, too excited for the occasion, like it often is. Monty takes her hand and squeezes it, which means *chill, babe*.

She pulls her hand away from Monty's and asks Anna, "Do you find my husband fuckable? I mean, in a situation where we're not married, and you see him at a bar or a club or wherever?"

"Jesus, Sage," Monty says and downs the rest of his bourbon.

She sees him sweating a little. She shakes her hair back and sits taller, counts to three, looks over at the pool where, earlier, she connected lilies to palm-sized plastic buoys and floated them in the water. In the glass wall of the living room, the reflected lilies resemble desiccated sea creatures. Last night, unable to sleep, she'd watched a documentary about an octopus. It had moved in such an implausible way across the ocean floor. The octopus intrigued her, this idea of being the thing that draws the eye, that surprises someone. She'd recently walked around her house with a piece of masking tape across her forehead for a whole weekend afternoon to see if anyone, her husband or sons, would notice, but no one had looked at her face at all.

Something slams against the living room's wall of glass, and the four of them startle. Monty starts to get up. He is always the one who gets up. Sage waits to see if things settle before she runs to the scene of a spill or a noise that doesn't make sense.

Sage hears the kids laugh from inside the house, so the noise was likely a wet Nerf ball because that is a game her kids like to play: get Nerf ball wet, throw ball against wall of glass in living room, laugh hysterically. Even more funny if Sage gets dampened and then level 100 funny if the wet foam hits Sage in the ass.

Anna and Haru have one child, fourteen-year-old Elena: black nails, midriff shirt, pierced bellybutton, big jeans. Sage's kids are ten and twelve, skaters who take boards onto canyon roads and come home to watch YouTubers pulling pranks and shouting. She worries they are not at all nuanced, but then she and Monty probably aren't either.

When she'd first been pregnant, she'd tricked herself into thinking motherhood would involve leading a troupe of smiling people from farmer's market to beach and then back home where they'd laugh and lounge on soft blankets and drift easily into sleep. Her own mother hadn't mustered that response from her children, Sage and her two brothers. She'd been cold and often absent. But Sage had wanted to be different, and mainly she had been. Now, though, the former versions of her kids, the soft kids, the sweet, smiling ones who might stand on her lap or hold onto her when they couldn't sleep, those kids were gone completely.

"Where were we?" Anna says. She dabs whipped cream off some remaining shards of pistachio brittle and lets it rest on her tongue for a second. "Your husband? If the conditions were right, sure," Anna says. "He's an appealing man, but then you know that. Okay, Haru, you ask someone now."

It's a dumb game, Sage knows. Looking bored by it is the move. Sage lights another cigarette. She lets the smoke out as slowly as she can. The coyotes are farther away now, but she can still hear them.

Haru pours more wine in their glasses. "Truth or dare," Haru says, looking at Sage. He's wearing one of those plaid short-sleeved shirts with snaps for buttons that looks one part indie and one part *I work at a cycling store*. Monty would never.

Sage does the slow blink back at him that she'd used years ago as a waitress on groups of businessmen who would tip more if she acted that way: moody, quiet, a little bit simple. One time, one of those men was Monty. She likes to remember being at his old place, a whole floor downtown, no walls, after food truck tacos and fucking, how she was someone who could stand on the bed in her underwear thinking, *Look at me, I'm what you want*.

"Truth," Sage says to Haru. She knows from seeing the philosophy and nature books in Anna and Haru's living room, that Haru is less of a dare and more of a truth kind of person.

"This isn't that interesting," he says, but he holds himself straight and leans forward in a way that means he does find himself interesting. "But what are your dealbreakers? Like I could say if someone doesn't read, it's over. Or if someone won't hike or take road trips or whatever."

All tame things. Sage doesn't need a 101 on dealbreakers. She could say something tame too, but instead she says, "If someone doesn't go down on me, that's a dealbreaker."

It's not the kind of thing she'd say normally in front of new people. She tries to look unbothered, though.

It's enough to make both Haru and Monty feel a little turned on, but not so much to make Monty uncomfortable because, really, it's a compliment to him, an indirect way of saying something about his skill or willingness or both.

Here's the thing: Sage knows Haru is not a man who would refuse to go down on someone. Two weeks after Anna and Haru moved in, Sage, upon seeing Haru ride his expensive bike up the driveway, walked down the path between their houses barefoot in one of Monty's long t-shirts and her swimming suit bottoms and asked Haru, "Is Anna here? I wanted to see how everything was with the house." This was in the garden where the hammock stretched between two trees, and the outdoor table was one she and Monty had picked up for too much money at someone's estate sale back before kids, when they did things like that together. Haru said, "Oh, Anna," and then, "she's teaching. She has one of those days, four courses right in a row. Brutal," which was when Sage took off her shirt and threw it onto the table. Monty was gone for a three-day business trip, the kids were at school, and she wanted a man she didn't know to see her for something she really wasn't. When she didn't feel terrible after, it confirmed something she'd wondered about related to her own capacity for meanness, or maybe about her own ability to feel nothing at all. Maybe she'd always been that way, or maybe self-erasure was a necessary tool of parenting.

Sage looks over at Haru, and he looks away. It's impossible to know who to be after having children. You're not who you were, but you're not new either.

"Okay, my turn," Monty says. "Haru, truth or dare?"

"Truth," Haru says. "No, wait. Dare."

Sage can see her younger son inside the living room messing with the stereo. Anna doesn't look toward the house, Sage notices. Anna's daughter, a teenager, is her own almost self-sustaining world bubble now. It was odd to be beyond the times of high and constant child need that are the first years of raising humans, to be able to sit in a chair for an elongated period, and feel unfamiliar to yourself, but to know also that the time when they will leave is coming faster, sooner. Her own mother might have said, "You can't win."

Monty scrapes his chair forward and puts his forearms on the table. "Okay, let's see your scars," Monty says to Haru. "Maybe that's not exactly a dare, but what scars do you have?"

"I don't have many, some road rash stuff from cycling, some places where I had stitches." He starts unsnapping his shirt, and Sage presumes Monty will go next, will use his question to Haru as an entry point for discussing his own scars, of which there are many, the knife wound below his rib cage on the right or his bicep where a dog's teeth shredded his skin, his road map to his own masculinity.

For a minute, the two men stand on the stone terrace pulling their shirts off. Anna raises her eyebrows.

"If we're getting undressed," Anna says, "Let's get in the pool."

Sage and Anna are the same age, or close, but Anna seems like someone who went to boarding school. Every word is precise. But she's also languid. *Is that the word*, Sage wonders. She thinks it is.

"Are we done with truth or dare, then?" Haru says when they are all in the water. Anna's bra is a bright yellow lace. Her underwear is lavender. Her breasts are small but also buoyant.

Had someone suggested earlier to Sage that they would end up in the pool in their underwear, it would have surprised her, but it didn't feel as strange as she might have thought. The water was warm from the heater, and she was drunk enough that she could lean back, look up at some filmy cloud passing over the moon, and for a minute not feel the pulse of want or worry or maybe melancholy.

"I guess we're done," Anna says, "But what's next?"

"Actually," Sage says, "I have a story." She drinks the rest of her drink and sets the glass on the tile at the edge of the pool. "I heard this at the gym. This woman was talking to her friend while we were all waiting for a class. She told this whole long thing while we were sitting there. It's fucked up. But it's kind of sexy." She hates the word sexy. It's one of those words that always feels false coming out of her mouth.

Haru sits on the pool's steps, and Monty leans against the pool wall closest to the house. Anna treads water close to Sage.

"This woman," Sage says, "she was walking in the neighborhood. You know those women, bored in the day and wandering. She comes upon one of her neighbors in his yard. They don't know each other well, apparently, even though they live sort of close. But she goes up to him to say hi or whatever and then takes off her shirt, unprompted, and, I mean, who knows what this man is thinking in a situation like that? Maybe he's stunned. Maybe he's grateful. Or maybe he's panicking."

"I don't know about this, babe, this doesn't sound real, who told you this?" Monty says.

"Yeah, seriously. I call bullshit," Haru says. He's doing something Sage recognizes, a stage trick where you look at someone's forehead instead of right in the eyes.

"This woman at the gym. I don't know. It seemed convincing at the time. Should I keep going?"

Monty gives her a look, climbs out, grabs a bottle of tequila from the bar cart, drinks, and passes it over to Haru.

"Yes," Anna says. "Keep going. I want to hear."

One of the kids inside has turned on the projector, and Sage can see silvery, large-eyed aliens reflected in the glass. Her kids are old enough that she doesn't have to worry they will fall down the stairs, choke, or crash through the plate glass. They are safe in the house. The next step for them is to be unsafe out in the world, skateboarding, strangers, weed. "Don't worry, the world will teach them," is something her mother used to say about her brothers, and she thinks of this line when she's worried her boys are being shitty or bossy or rude. The world doesn't teach everyone, though, because there are people walking around, untaught: douchebags, psychopaths, grifters.

"So, what happened? Half-naked woman in a yard?" Anna asks. Sage is close enough to see the bumps on Anna's upper arms where the breeze has turned her skin cold.

"Okay, so I guess she strips all the way down, and then they go at it, right there in the yard. It's shielded by shrubs or trees or whatever, I assume. But as it's happening, the woman, I guess she starts to be repulsed by it, starts to hate herself a little, not for what she's doing, which is maybe what she should feel, but more for being so disengaged from it all."

Monty scoops the lilies and their buoys out of the water and lines them up on the tile deck. Haru looks down into the dark beyond the pool.

"I feel like I've heard a similar story, like maybe from my roommate in grad school," Anna says. She floats so her toes are up above the water. Her toenail polish is silver. It looks like a small herd of Amazonian beetles has affixed themselves to her feet.

Grad school, Sage thinks, *of course.*

Anna's body is beautiful. When Sage turns, she sees her husband looking at it, and he smiles at Sage because this is something they usually bond on: their love of looking at women's bodies. They can be at an event somewhere, something for his work, and they can stand with drinks and assess everyone. *Her? Yes. Her? No. Her? Fuck yes.*

"Anyway, that's it," Sage says. "Apparently she put her clothes on, walked home, and went from being a woman fucking in a stranger's yard to, I guess, maybe being a woman getting her kids a snack after school or whatever women around here do on any given weekday."

They all go quiet, and the pool heater hums out its hymn of white noise. Sage remembers that day. She didn't actually go home and make snacks. She ran the hottest bath and spent who knows how long staring at the dried petals on the skylight and thinking *my life is easy, I am ridiculous* like a mantra.

Here's the other thing: a few days after Anna and Haru moved into Sage and Monty's rental house, the house where Sage and Monty had lived when Sage was first pregnant and the larger house was being gutted, Sage came home from kid drop-off on a day she assumed Monty was at work. She walked straight back to the bedroom, her bedroom, and there were Anna and Monty, his pants at his ankles, shirt still on. Anna was unclothed, mainly, but in that way of someone who'd gone from zero to fucking in five seconds. Her bra, bronze with thin straps, was pushed up above her tits but not undone in the back so that it almost looked like a part of a cracked shell. She was up against the wall that separated the bedroom and bathroom, and, in that moment, Sage could think only of the paint swatches they'd taped to that wall before Monty decided on the saturated navy.

It wasn't that Sage felt proprietary. What bothered her was that whatever fantasy woman Monty had constructed in his head to stand for her, for Sage, that version had been chipped away by all of the day-to-day things that make one kind of love richer and more and another kind of love muted and less. After seeing the two of them, Sage backed down the hall and got into her car and drove to the trailhead and walked up and up to the peak until she wasn't sad and was instead strategically nothing in all the ways life to that point, girlhood, womanhood, motherhood, had taught her to be.

When the kids finally come outside, it has to be after midnight. The candles on the farm table have gone out. No neighbor's music filters up the canyon.

Anna and Haru's daughter gets down the steps first. Her eyeliner is smeared below her lower eyelids. Sage's sons look like they just woke up. They rub their eyes and shake their shaggy hair back from their faces.

There's a certain type of Instagram mom who wears leopard running tights and drives a car as long and wide as a pontoon boat and hashtags every post with #boymom, who expects all the wrong things of their sons: don't cry, you're fine, grow some balls, hit him where it hurts. Sage has worked to teach her boys differently, to let them talk and cry, but she's not so sure it will matter. Her boys stand by the pool and stare down at the grownups like they're not human at all, like they're pandas or tigers, like they're no one they know.

Sage is drunk and leaning against the pool wall by the stairs where Haru is sitting in the shallow part of the water, and Monty is where? Sage can see what she thinks is Monty touching Anna under the water in the pool's deep end.

She looks from Monty to the spot where her boys stand, and she can see they see this too. Anna and Monty move apart.

Her boys stare at each other. They aren't hers, really. She knows this. She's a shepherd or steward for a blip, and soon they'll be in beds they bought with their own money and fucking people they don't know but think they know or don't even want to know. Maybe they'll think to be gentle when they are in beds with other people, maybe they'll think other people require it. Regardless, they aren't hers, and they'll look at her soon with disdain or disregard or sadness. Still, she wants to jump from the pool, to be gauze over their eyes, to usher them back to earlier childhood when they were different and so was she.

Her older son is the first to pick up one of the buoyed lilies, and he chucks it right at Monty. It's heavier than you might think, and it makes a loud noise when it misses Monty and hits the water. Monty laughs, but it's one of those laughs that starts strong and dissolves, and then the only noise is pool burble. Haru and Anna's daughter grabs two of the lilies and throws them as hard as she can toward her own mother.

All three kids gather rocks from the succulent planter and hurl them into the pool. They're small stones, pebbles, really, but they hurt when they land. Monty is yelling at them, "Cut this shit out," but the rocks keep coming.

It occurs to Sage that she should climb out of the pool and run around the house, away from all of them, up the narrow road toward the peak again, with the snap of her neighbors' motion lights illuminating her bare feet as she goes, everything strange and wild and dark, and time undoing itself so she's the Sage of five years ago, ten, fifteen, twenty. She doesn't leave the pool, though.

Her younger boy picks up a wine glass from one of the small wooden tables between two lounge chairs and throws it toward the pool. It hits the railing and breaks into pieces, and Sage feels a sliver lodging in her fingertip. She watches the blood bloom out around her in the water, pretty if she doesn't think about it, almost like those gelatin sculptures, where people inject elaborate flowers or patterns into clear domes.

Her boys look rageful but also slightly broken, and Monty is about to climb out and do who knows what as punishment.

Sage sucks on her own bleeding finger, and her mouth fills with metallic liquid. She gives Monty a look that says *don't*, goes to wrap towels around her boys, pulls a dirty cloth napkin around her finger, says quick goodbyes to Anna and Haru and their daughter who walk down the path dripping water and with clothes bundled in front of them. Sage sweeps the mess from the pool deck, goes to the desk in the kitchen to email the pool cleaner before she forgets, loads the dishwasher, gets waters for the boys and sets them on their bedside tables before turning out their lights, finds Monty already asleep in the chair by his record player, and walks through the dark, quiet house with all its uncurtained wall-sized windows and then, finally, sits on the edge of the tub with tweezers to pull the needle of glass from her finger. The sliver plinks when it hits the trashcan's bottom, and she closes her eyes.

This is it, Sage thinks. *This is motherhood.*

Wizards of the Coast

Ari's ninth birthday party is held at a castle in the Holly-wood Hills. Even though he hates crowds and people in general, he loves Hermione Granger, so his parents requisitioned a set designer to turn a rented 1930s home built in a castle style into Hogwarts. There are actors playing McGonagall and Dumbledore, and his mother's friend who used to play professional basketball is dressed as Hagrid and drinking a martini in the corner by the stained-glass picture window.

The party is mostly his mother's friends, because she is the one with friends, and some of them have brought their children. A makeup artist has etched scars onto their foreheads. They are draped over by invisibility cloaks made of gray tulle, and they are being sorted (Gryffindor by choice for most and Slytherin for the self-professed rule-breakers) by a sorting hat manipulated by a puppeteer who once worked with the Muppets.

Ari wears his Harry Potter glasses and a tie and cardigan under his tulle invisibility cloak and leans against a wall turning his fingers ragged with hangnails. When his mother's friend, Steve, the set designer everyone calls Twiggy, leans against the wall next to him and tells him the caterers have hidden the excess candy in a person-sized dumbwaiter on the second floor, Ari follows him not so much for a love of candy but because somewhere else sounds better than where he is.

Ari watches the backs of Twiggy's low brown boots as they ascend the stairs. The carpeting is thick and patterned in a way that someone must have thought looked royal but really looks more like it belongs in a hotel in Nevada. Twiggy pauses at the top, turns around and *shhs* Ari, even though Ari has not made a sound. There is not a child more capable of absolute quiet than he is. At least that is what his mom told him on mornings when they sat with tea on the terrace watching birds fling themselves through the mist over the hot tub while downtown LA hovered like a Lego construct on the horizon. "We are here but not *of here*, somehow," his mother said to him and held tight to whatever special and powerful stone hung from a leather cord around her neck. He always thought he knew what she meant when she said that—that their superpower was to skate above the top of any scene while remaining physically there, to blanch from it what was needed while staying unaffected by anything clawed or pronged or painful. It was a talent, and she had bequeathed it to him, and it meant that when she looked at him, they knew, even if his dad did not. They just knew.

The dumbwaiter's white painted door has a knob made of brass and carved into the shape of a dragon's head. When Twiggy opens it, it doesn't creak as Ari expects it to. Someone downstairs yells, "Gryffindor" and kids cheer, and grownups tap mimosa flutes together. The dumbwaiter is big enough for two people to sit close in a quiet and dark space. Ari's invisibility cloak settles into a scratchy fluff pushed in around him. He presses up against clear plastic bags of sparkling candy: rock candy colorful and clinging to sticks, candy eyeballs with blue, green, and brown irises, their pupils staring out questions, simple candy fruits in the shapes of things that grow on rowed trees outside.

When Twiggy runs one fingernail across the knuckles of Ari's right hand, and he feels it leave a light chalk line, he closes his eyes and thinks of this week's yoga mantra, the one his mother has whispered to him while they downward dogged on their side-by-side purple mats in the early morning: inside, you are made of flowers. Repeat.

The drive down the canyon is always the same, the same hurtling turns through the cliffs and spiked plants that can go weeks without water. Kate says a few things into the quiet world of the backseat, but Gigi and George ignore Kate and text each other, the shadows moving over their faces as the car turns and turns again, and then suddenly Kate sees water in the distance. Somehow the blue after the canyon is always a surprise.

Kate had one daughter, Gigi, a tiny thirteen-year-old with blonde hair she could sit on who dressed exclusively in clothes meant for a ten-year-old boy and could talk for five minutes solid and then go away for hours and say nothing at all. Georgina came to live with them three years ago, after her own mother, thinned out by pills, disappeared north. She was going to Arcata, she'd told George. She'd be back after an overnight or maybe two. For almost two weeks, George, then ten, had remained in her Venice apartment by herself, living on toast and canned things until Gigi brought her home. George had gotten a few texts from her mother those first months but then nothing.

Gigi and George didn't wear bikinis. They didn't play beach volleyball. They didn't text boys. They didn't have Instagram. They didn't believe in Snapchat. Most of their late afternoons were spent among the rocks and yuccas and snakes of the few acres of uncharted land below their house, an adobe behind a stone and iron gate. They tracked coyotes, made maps, found and claimed an abandoned shack. They had once stuck a sharpened stick straight through the head of a Western rattlesnake, or so they'd told Kate.

At first, Kate had been elated by the friendship. Gigi was an odd child. It was good for her to have George. Now, though, Kate felt eclipsed in her own life, tangential, and it bothered her more than she wanted to admit.

They are ten minutes late to the birthday party and stuck behind a slow-moving pickup with a surfer sitting in the back, his wetsuit puddled at his ankles, banging his head to music that pours from the truck's open windows: "Voodoo Child."

The birthday party is for her old friend Lucas's son, Ari. She'd run into Lucas a few weeks before at one of the northern beaches where she usually never saw anyone she knew. She was in grad school when they'd first met. She was a TA, a bookstore employee, aspirational but also drunk a lot of the time. And he'd been a musician, touring cross-country in a van full of alcoholics in vintage western shirts. Kate was one of many road hookups, and their on-and-off thing lasted two years before he stopped calling her completely.

When she'd first moved from the Midwest to Topanga and started coming to Malibu, to Zuma, and farther up the coast to Leo Carillo, she had expected only a certain kind of woman lying on those Malibu beaches. In her mind, the woman wore a vibrant bikini, had surgical skin, and was twenty-eight. In fact, the beaches were populated by teenagers in t-shirts and shorts screaming each time a wave knocked them down and plain-seeming mothers in big button-ups or one-pieces who sat in circles on blankets and ate food out of plastic containers.

There was nothing to fear at such a beach. When Kate sat a few body lengths down from a man who turned out to be Lucas and looked out at him from under her straw hat, she didn't recognize him at first. It was one of those moments she'd found herself having regularly in her forties: looking at a man, thinking *he is cute for an older guy* and then realizing he was her age. Each time, it was this weird soft slap. When he walked over to her, she was relieved to see he looked as old as she did, not old really, but with the slightly sad look of people in their forties, their eyes puffy and lips downturned at the edges.

"Here we go again," he said as he sat down on the sand next to her. She instantly both liked and distrusted him all over again.

"After only the briefest of interludes," she said and shifted her hat back and her shirt down.

He had discarded the snap-front shirts and was wearing, instead, faded jeans, a plain t-shirt.

After ten minutes, she had an invitation to his son's upcoming birthday party, and she knew the following: they were both parents; they were both married, but loosely and after more than a decade; he no longer played music; he now wrote and produced, and pop stars recorded his bad songs off of which he made a lot of money; he was

still a classic asshole, but like any classic asshole, he had
his appeal.

When they finally arrive, Kate parks and leads them
into the house's living room, and Gigi and George immediately head up the stairs with a wide bowl of cumin-dust-
ed popcorn.

Kate, seeing only strangers, small Harrys and Hermiones
and their parents, walks into the backyard garden and
stands on the brick path surrounded by topiary animals.
The garden is *Downton Abbey*-esque. In the corner, a koi
pond encircled by boxwoods is shaded by a flowering tree
whose petals hang open like small, wanting mouths.

Since running into Lucas on the beach, she has brought
up several Google images of him from the last ten years,
but the one that sticks with her features Lucas and his wife
and child at a farmers' market, all three of them wearing
white and holding pomegranates in each hand and all with
fingernails painted in a rainbow of pinks. When he walks
out of the house and down the brick path toward her, she
sees his fingernails are unpainted.

In the past week, Lucas has texted Kate more than a hundred times. It's clichéd, and she's heard a million podcasts
about this very thing: falling into a messaging relationship
with an old boyfriend, traveling back to being not a wife,
not a mother.

She stops Lucas on the path behind the flowering tree
and pulls his hand into her pants in a way that fails to
recognize any before or after. Fuck the binding expectations of monogamy. She isn't a sociopath, but oh to have
a moment without care or consequence. It comes to her
far too easily.

◆

Popcorn makes a snowstorm at their feet. The huge silver bowl is empty, and their faces are dusted with cumin and salt. They are on the third story of a house that is used solely for events and no real living, a house no one should have built, avoiding a *Harry Potter* party because even though Gigi and George have read and reread *Harry Potter*, they are thirteen and no longer children. The room is vaulted, and the windows are stained glass filled with the shapes of fruit and maidens. The walls are hung with tapestries that look like they have come straight from TJ Maxx. There is nothing legitimately castle about the room, but from a distance, yes, with eyes squinted, there is a castle-like effect.

"There are castles," Gigi says, picking popcorn from the floor and throwing pieces into George's mouth. "And then there are structures that aspire to castledom but fall..."

"So short," George finishes.

On their drive down from the canyon, they'd seen him: Devendra. A twenty-something man dressed in a sheet, like Jesus in running shoes, at the side of the road at the last turn-out on the canyon. A military backpack leaning against one shin, and his thumb pointed to the sky.

"It was him by the road, wasn't it?" George asks, popcorn still in her teeth. Her brown hair is in the tight braids of a younger child. She has the very beginnings of breasts, and it's clear from her height and thinness that it's probably going to stay that way.

"'Twas. Devendra, yes. Of our canyon shack. Of the dead snake. The very one. What was with the Jesus robe?" Gigi sits up and smooths her t-shirt. She pulls her light hair into a rope that she twists repeatedly around her wrist until she's caught her own head in a vice. She lets it unfurl.

"Who knows? Maybe he thinks he's some kind of Messiah figure. Or maybe he doesn't care about clothes and is going for convenience? A million potential maybes, really," George says. She had a mother. She doesn't have a mother. She has Gigi's mother. She even sometimes calls Gigi's mother: mother, mom, in the middle of the night once, mommy.

They are right at the edge of really thinking of boys, of huddling with them in dark rooms, of rolling on beds with them, but they aren't there yet. There is a future they know is coming, and it's amorphous and a little bit terrifying. There will be the stripping away of things, the giving away. For now, they love each other in a way and with a comfort they might not ever have again.

"Devendra, Devendra, Devendra!" Gigi is almost shouting, and George puts her hand over her mouth. Gigi spits chewed popcorn onto it, and George screams, and then they are actually and truly rolling on the floor, on the scratchy carpeting, laughing.

The two girls are subjects. It is all an experiment. It is not an experiment. It is beyond terms or titles. People will want to apply terms and titles. But he will push beyond that. No ephemera. No preset roles. No demarcation of weather. No rainy days. No sunny days. Just presence and continuance but not even that. Not even those words. One has yellow hair and laughs less nervously than the other. One has brown hair and had once sat in the shack in the canyon and looked to the window and, he imagines, wondered about the absence of glass in the frame. But he doesn't want those descriptors. And he doesn't want their sounds to be differentiated in his mind. And he doesn't *want* want. None of it. He is on Canyon Road, and his feet are sunburnt in the running shoes he found, but he is unaware, or at least mainly so. He wants only to observe the red lines that circle his ankles and note omnisciently, objectively, that there are red sunburn lines on his ankles. But he is not there yet. At least not as there as he wants to be. And there is the want again. And that is the problem. Or one of the problems. But he wants to be above problems. Wants not to want. Again.

The one with the brown hair and the one with the yellow hair came with a dead snake on a stick to the shack, and he cleaned it and cooked it and ate it. To be beyond food would be a thing, but he is not that impractical. When he cared about things like skin, he paid someone to tattoo colorful snakes wrapping around both of his forearms. That was when he lived with a bed and a microwave and bought food in a building that separated food into aisles and categories and appealed to buyers by using health claims and color. He has found that he can subsist on yucca and rye and mountain dandelion and food discarded by people that he scavenges from bins in the dark. It's always enough, and it's the least of his concerns.

The road from the canyon is a snake. He could pick it up and shake it flat. He could wind it more. He could cover it with yucca points. On the road's shoulder, he is at the still point of two worlds. He imagines he sees the two girls in a car that almost hits him before curving away—the subjects—he should get beyond girl, boy, human, creature. All of it. His name is ridiculous. Devendra. He gave it to himself when he cared about the snakes on his forearms. After a singer he admired. What was he before? John, Josh, Jared, something common. But now to be beyond names. It would be a thing.

The car that stops for him is the green color of a ripe pear. It's a small car that makes claims to fuel efficiency on its bumper. He normally eschews cars. But that word tries too hard. He should rephrase. He normally avoids cars. He avoids cars. Simplify. The man who drives the car likes to think he is beyond the mundanity and restrictions of suburban life. He talks about chickens and bee keeping and solar. The man's hands are clean. He is clean. His odor is that of someone who has running water in the place where he lives.

The house where the green car parks is stone and rises into spires. The man unloads covered platters from the back of the car. "I'm so late," he says and gestures to the open hatchback. "Help me get these in, cupcakes," he says, and just like that he follows the man in the open back door of the castle house. The kitchen is tick and swirl, and the windows are crying color. Once he carried a surfboard with a rainbow spilling down its center. Once his mother ran her fingers down his bare back over and over while he fell asleep in July in his un-airconditioned childhood apartment. All of the spines and all of the centers. All of the days.

The back stairs are a caterpillar. The back stairs beckon. How should he say it without oversaying it? He walks up the stairs and then another flight, past a window shaped like a window in a ship, and then he is in an open room, and there are the subjects. It is beyond coincidence. He doesn't believe in the universe as a force in the way that the yoga juice women talk about it. He doesn't believe in being led to anything. He believes in matter, in atoms that work in combination, and in randomness as an opposite, in gravity, if in anything.

He doesn't want the two subjects to be naked in the way that a man with a criminal past would want young girls to be naked. He wants them to be naked to be untethered in the way of animals in the canyon. It is for them. He doesn't want to touch them. He wants them to feel their skin colliding with air and understand that clothes are a construct. He would never touch them. He eschews touch. No. Simplify. He touches not. He does not touch. At night he sleeps on the wood floor of the shack flat on his back with his feet separated, his hands wide to his sides almost touching the wooden walls.

He has stood in front of a train and wished for the moment of impact. The dust of the soul. But there is no soul, you idiot. The dust of motion and immobility together for a moment before dispersing. The subjects are cool skinned in front of him. The two girls. Their hair in curtains. Brown. Yellow. His mother pushed his hair from his face on so many days. She rubbed her finger on his hand when he was crying. He didn't know where she was anymore, and he didn't want to. He didn't. The colors from the sun through the window glass become stains on their skin. They look at each other. The one with the yellow hair gets pink at her cheeks. The one with the brown hair looks to her feet and reaches for the hand of the one with the yellow hair. The sun hits the windows. They are glowing with color, and the room is quiet. So many things erased. So many more things coming. He leaves them like that.

Right or wrong, when Ari thinks of sex—at twelve, at twenty, at sixty—this will be home to Ari. This dark box of the dumbwaiter with light darting through the cracks and making the bulk bags of candy he uses as pillows into plastic-wrapped gemstones. Twiggy's hands making small circles around Ari's chest and abdomen. It is candy, those circles, and while he knows it is wrong and no matter how many therapists try to persuade him otherwise over how many decades, he will never be talked out of its beauty and softness, its quaint pre-penetrative simplicity. Desire superseding the act the end-all for him, the act itself not nothing, but not the thing for him really.

No matter who the man, no matter what the room. The moment before was the moment. Repeat.

Edward Abbey Walks into a Bar

When someone I've been dating off and on for a year calls from the beer cooler of the liquor store where he works and says he has a gun to his head and is going to kill himself, really, because I don't care enough, really, I never did, it's probably best not to embark on a road trip with him the next day. It's better to text him *I don't think I can go actually, I'm so sorry* and turn my phone off and go to sleep, after which he leaves a series of messages:

He's sorry.

He's really sorry.

He's slept it off and cleaned out his truck.

He sold his guitars to his roommates for gas money, and he has a tent from his brother.

He took five hundred from the deposit envelope in the office of the liquor store.

He's making it to Vancouver where he'll build a driftwood shack by the water.

He definitely put the gun back in the gun safe under the counter at the liquor store, beneath the tiny bottles of cheap whiskey that people buy when they've scraped together enough coins, and they want to get drunk enough not to feel the Kansas weather.

But I go anyway. I put the vintage costume-wear that is my wardrobe and is inappropriate for camping into a backpack and decide to start smoking because why not? During my only two years of college, I stewed about climate change and the swamps of plastics joining forces, but now everything felt in decline. No amount of refraining and recycling was going to un-strangle the waterfowl or stop the fires or hold back the oceans. There had been some small peace in imagining these efforts mattered, that each recycled newspaper was a direct trade for a patch of rainforest re-sprouting, tree branches reaching out to each other in some dance of commensalism to make us forget the pained state of the sky.

May your trails be crooked, winding, lonesome, dangerous, and leading to the most amazing view. At least that's what Edward Abbey said. At least that's what the small, bearded Elizabethan-seeming man who ran the nature essay class I took in my sophomore year of college wrote on the board on the first day. As if no one in the room had to go work second shift at Kwik Shop later that day or make artful lattes for the mothers of toddlers. The professor told us we should explore like Abbey, be untethered and unconcerned, and he spit a little when he talked about Annie Dillard never traveling too far but instead making her small circles around one house in one place and, he said, "pretending to like it."

Western Kansas is simply hot with monstrous white sci-fi windmills poking up out of slight yellow-green hills. We listen to too much Brian Eno and then stop for food. We sit at picnic tables outside of a McDonalds and smoke and share a giant Dr. Pepper. Under the tables, the grass is bristly and brown at the tips. Flies swarm our ankles. A child hangs from her knees on one of the metal bars of a play structure that belongs to a previous generation. The girl closes her eyes and two small dogs approach and lick her upside-down face. The boyfriend, Tim, drinks the last of the Dr. Pepper and pulls his shirt up to scratch the heat rash that has formed at the waistline of his jeans and there, of course, is the gun.

For reference: my father owned a BB gun he pointed at squirrels in the attic but never shot. For reference: when I was twelve, I drove with my mother across half the country to Central Park where, among nearly a million strangers, we begged in chants for nuclear disarmament. I started a pacifist club at my high school. I told the punks who were my friends to stop smashing into each other at shows, knowing they would mock me for it, knowing they would presume I was missing the point. But I did still cut my upper thighs with glass shards and razors. I was not immune to the lure of violence. But, for reference: this gun did bother me from the beginning.

We camp on the side of a hill off I-91 in Utah near Arches National Park. We set the tent up in a rocky and unprotected spot not at all meant for camping. It's freezing once the sun drops out. I go in and out of dreams. In the one dream I remember, Edward Abbey pipe bombs a row of RVs. He's spent months in a lab he built in a cave, and he's emerged with an eradicative potion, "intended to combat modernity," he shouts and then starts shredding all that is even remotely contemporary until the land is sheared cliffside and wild radish, no through roads anywhere to be seen.

In the morning, Tim and I dismantle the tent and drive to Arches. Even though Edward Abbey opposed it, a road winds through Arches National Park. Tourists look out tinted windows at Delicate Arch. They slow down to point. They eat crackers out of cellophane and direct their eyes toward improbable assemblages of orange rock. "This is like being close to God," I hear one of them say when we walk past one of the RVs with its half-open window. Tim rolls his eyes.

My grandmother, though once Jewish, had converted to Christian Science and convinced me the devil could take up occupancy inside of a person and spin illness out of negativity. It's exactly this, that chemical spread of badness, that my grandmother imagined, but no longer entombed in bodies, now spreading through the land.

My grandmother used a cigarette holder at parties. She didn't bake. She ate Grape-Nuts without milk for the rigor of it. But then, she also taught me things like: *stand up straight. Look pretty. Be quiet. Let him do it. Smile. He wants to do it.* And for all the years up to this one, I had.

This is not a road trip story. There are no antics. This is a story about aging out of the frivolity of twenty-one, twenty-two, twenty-three, etc., in a dying world.

When Bruce Springsteen interrupts Clarence Clemons to scream/sing/whisper about the Badlands and finding a face that's not looking through him, it feels personal. Tim and I are driving west through Nevada on the "Loneliest Highway in America," and the world is a salt flat with sage

weaving through sand and mountains on burned-out mountains mocking my desire for a public bathroom or some food
that isn't orange cheese crackers in a plastic jacket.

A campground sits at the spot where the Loneliest
Highway merges with the interstate near the western
edge of Nevada.

"Civilization," Tim says with sarcasm when we unload the
tent and erect it in its designated rectangle. The desert is
still pervasive, but this is not the campground of Abbey's
dreams. We didn't pack in; we drove right up to a camp-
site with a grill planted like a tree next to it. In a stucco
building near our tent, people microwave frozen pizzas
and play bingo.

When it gets dark and cold and I can't sleep, I start seeing
things. My ghost of desert past chanting *Pretty girl, pretty
girl* while standing with folded arms in front of a gathering
of cacti. *Pretty girl* as in: Look good. Don't take up space.
Ghost of desert past in knock-off Doc Martens and a flow-
ered vintage baby doll dress then at a bar or a party and
this or that boy will be forever trying to grab her breasts
without asking.

My ghost of desert future will be much older than Bruce
of *Darkness on the Edge of Town* but younger than aging
stadium Bruce and in the passenger seat of a car passing
the Bean Flat Rest Area, Highway 50, Nevada, twenty-some
years later and with my two kids in the back seat eating
bulk candy and fighting. Yelp says pizza is the only option,
and in the town, there will be a cemetery right in the middle, its green carpet lawn a green that shouldn't happen in
Nevada, and I'll hate my husband less than the day before.
My ghost of desert future will put "Hang Fire" on because
it reminds me of something I want to grab onto, I'm not

sure what, and my ten-year-old son will say, "Hang fire stands for a slow plan," and I'll think, this is certainly the slow plan. A year before, Tim will have Facebook messaged from Reno where he appeared to have married a woman who "lived to cycle" and where apparently, he only did a year in prison because the whole thing with the gun in the bar was accidental, and where he worked in radio sales, which he said was a dying industry.

My ghost of desert present is at the campground an hour east of Reno in a Walmart tent. By one A.M., it's forty-five degrees and we're both awake and shivering, so we give in, shove the tent into the back of the truck without fully disassembling it, and drive down the block to a motel slash casino with a billboard that promises "showgirls" in pink silhouette.

My grandmother died in a two-piece nylon track suit that looked stolen from 1980s David Byrne. She was eighty-seven but still barricaded the door of her assisted living room to keep the aides out for over an hour because what did they know about how to pray illness and maybe even old age away? She sat against the door in the one room that was hers, surrounded by her Japanese pottery, her brass-framed family photos, the water-spotted folded letters from her long-dead brother. That door-blocking was her last fuck you to all that people expected of her, and of course she looked good doing it. When she sat on the floor and died right there, there was no floating away of the soul from the body. There was no perfect garden. There was no puffy cloud moment. That was just it. The end, while outside the window, the last un-built-upon suburban field in a ten-mile radius boasted a pack of screeching starlings following each other above the grass in a frantic pattern of swoops and swirls. Heaven is a place where nothing ever happens. At least that's what David Byrne says.

Outer Reno is not the desert Edward Abbey imagined. Xfinity, strippers, International House of Pancakes, Bourbon Square. There is a feeling of hyperactivity before absolute dissolution. Will it come from civil war, boys with AR-15s stalking through Walmart parking lots finally summoned to the fight of their dreams? Will there be an end to currency? Will all the air conditioners time out until we're wandering in shredded clothes toward the still-cool pockets of pine forests?

Tim and I go to the bar by the motel, open 24/7, a place with dark wood paneling and the standard few very drunk men leaning over on bar stools. Tim and I sit through what feels like a Jukebox worth of bad new country. We drink several beers before Tim gets up to go to the bathroom. One of the drunk men moves onto his stool. Tim is a small man but strong, and when he comes back from the bathroom, drunk and deposed of his stool, he doesn't pause before pushing the man off.

Edward Abbey challenges Annie Dillard to a fist fight, but she is uninterested. She paces a square around a shed that's in the center of a field where mice have woven tunnels through tall grass. She wears tall boots made of something indestructible but somehow unchemical. Her hair covers her face, and she doesn't bring a hand up to pull it out of the way. She brushes Edward Abbey aside, though. She stalks. She wanders. She looks up. The sky changes. She wonders but not in a Jane Austen or Edna Pontellier way. There is no soft or uncertain contemplating. Her look is a razor. And then the gun goes off. Edward Abbey jumps. He angers. But Annie Dillard doesn't flinch. She knew this was coming. She has no interest in ranting. She's pulled a dead raccoon from a crawl space and thrown it in a creek for a water burial. She's eaten squirrel. She probably sees the future and keeps walking toward it anyway.

The gun is in Tim's hand, and that's no surprise. His face doesn't have time to startle. No one is dead, I can see that. My grandmother would say *mop up the blood, smile, fix it.* I can imagine my hand doing that, getting a towel from the bartender, waiting for the ambulance, reassuring the bleeding man, talking him down, convincing him it was an accident. Maybe then Tim and I would walk away unscathed and together. We'd turn the car east, buy a bungalow in the town where we'd started, get jobs, grow several kinds of peppers, become famous among our friends for our salsas.

Annie Dillard, however, would wipe her boot bottoms on the floor mat by the door and find a place for just her, so that's what I do: pretend I don't know Tim when the police come. I stand by the bar, wipe my hands on a square napkin, and walk out of the orange-painted metal door, past the block-long Ben's Discount Liquors, and keep going. It matters that I have been the keeper of the keys and the cash.

By eight A.M., I am in a small town by the ocean. By the next day, I have a job bussing tables at a brewery. I spend my days off on a beach where driftwood trunks bigger than trucks are covered with the carved initials of strangers, and there are more dogs than people. The shorn-off trees hang quietly on the cliff sides. Bees flicker through blackberry bushes.

Fifty years from now, the world will be the same but not. Knees will go. Hips will go. All the glass bottles will be broken, and their blue and green and brown shards, soft at the edges, will creep up on the sand the way the sea creatures we remember in dreams once did. Fish will be the stuff of tall tales. Edward Abbey will bellow and echo in all the orange canyons. We'll half-sleep through Annie Dillard's rubber-booted footsteps in the tall grass, and the glass fragments will stare up unblinking, like the washed-out eyes of the dead.

Corvids and Their Allies

Sasha Morningstar legally changed his name to Michael on his eighteenth birthday in the Mendocino County Courthouse while holding the hand of his younger sister, Moonbeam Lark, who, though thirteen and not old enough to change her name, now went exclusively by Hannah.

They had not been raised in the standard way of parents raising children. Rather, when he was five, Sasha, now Michael, was taken by his mother from the apartment they shared with his father at 25 Sutton Place in New York, overlooking the East River, and loaded into the back of a van and driven by strangers across the country. He remembered that journey in pieces, like a flipbook: sleeping with his leg against his mother's and his head against the van's metal back door, and looking out the small submarine window at the sky and the tops of tall things in some eastern city; his mother racing out of a gas station with an armload of boxes of Saltines, her hair snaking behind her head; stopping at the house of someone they maybe knew or maybe didn't know in the middle of a desert where they swam in a pool until they heard coyotes and the sun was completely down.

Where he ended up shouldn't have surprised him, but it did. Yes, his mother had often gone shoeless in the city, but the apartment they'd left had belonged to his father's parents and was heavy with their possessions: a grand piano, velvet curtains, a desk inlaid with gold. He had spent weekends on the window seat, leafing through a set of encyclopedias and looking out at the bridge over the river.

It was dark and late when the van pulled in front of a series of erratically constructed small houses in a northern California forest. He would later learn that the commune was started in 1968 as a conceptual art slash ecological project by a man who, at the time of their arrival on a Saturday night in 1973, was sitting on a deck surrounded by candles and crates of strawberries and snap peas that he was disentangling and putting into metal buckets, but slowly, so that each movement looked balletic. That night, he fell asleep on a long pillow near the man's bare feet.

Hannah née Moonbeam Lark was nothing then, one step beyond idea, implanted but with little growth. She would come later, as would several attempts at collective money making: a vegetarian sandwich delivery service that involved ritual assembly in their communal kitchen space and then van drives into town where they would go door to door with lunches wrapped in wax paper. A forestry service where both men and women shimmied up dying trees with chainsaws and none of the appropriate safety equipment.

He didn't like it always, but he was still all in. As he grew, he climbed the trees and did maintenance on the houses. He gathered moss for terrariums to sell at coastal art fairs. He picked blackberries by the ocean and helped convert them to jam on the woodstove. He watched his mother pair off with a series of men and then women and then men again, many of whom stayed for a few months only. He carried Hannah, when he was too small to do it at first, in a patchwork sling along the path that overlooked the ocean, and later she walked a few feet behind him while he pointed out to her caravans of sea lions sleeping on distant rocks. For some years, they were the only children, and then there were suddenly many babies. He forgot what he'd known about the city, about buses that exhaled gray air, about his father, about concentrations of human-made noise.

What happened shouldn't have surprised him. He was old enough to hear them planning, and he spent weeks trying to convince his mother, Evelyn, to leave the place instead, to walk out, to get on a bus, anything. She'd made him call her that for the first years there: Evelyn. Not Mom, not Mommy. Then she insisted he call her Seven, her maiden name though the patriarchy that required the switching of names when marrying as if property was ridiculous, she told him, and though Seven represented really her father and not her, she supposed it was as good a name as any, and she "preferred being numeric." Seven, then, it was, and if he defaulted in the night to Mom, when he was cold and younger and needed to use the outhouse and didn't want to go alone, she lay silent until he said it: "Seven, help."

Their scheme, the foxglove, the nightshade. Please, he told her so many times, no. There was no other world, he told her, when they were foraging on an October morning, no astral plane, no mystical beyond, no living as a star among stars. There was solid human form animated by an energy that, upon death, was simply and completely gone. His mother set down her canvas bag, sat cross-legged on a rug of pine needles, closed her eyes, and tipped her chin up without speaking. There were more than the expected number of ravens in the trees calling, and though the sun was out that day, the light barely made its way through the canopy.

He and his sister took the truck in the morning straight to the courthouse. It was the truck the older men used to drive the log roads and to wind inland at night to steal things from farms and vineyards. Sometimes they returned with live chickens in burlap and more than once an actual goat tied by rope to the truck bed.

He'd taken the bag of money from the drawer in the communal kitchen. Hannah, of course, had brought her bird book along with a lot of old and handmade clothes they later realized were embarrassing and not right for a world where people wore pink Izods and Hawaiian print shorts and leather jackets and shirts with bright words printed across them.

After, on that whole drive, on the roads through the hills to the courthouse and then across California, Nevada, and all the way to New York, they saw corvids everywhere, ravens and then, farther east, crows, and though neither would say it out loud, they both thought the birds were following them, shepherding.

He could remember reading something in a book about a world made new, and he decided on this as a mantra as they drove through the redwoods and then east, when the world went parched and colorless, and then trees again, and then suddenly all and completely orange. All of it in front of them: cities vertical with glass, employment maybe, a father, tan houses in rows in farm fields, love maybe, sex eventually, sadness of course, the future.

◆

Evelyn knows every plant, plants more than people. Elephanthead lousewort in small amounts only. False Solomon's seal berry edible high in vitamin C common in forests and thickets. Indian pipe/ghost plant white, stalky, edible, similar to asparagus but poisonous in quantity, eat sparingly. Miner's lettuce all parts of the plant, even the roots. Queenscup, yes. Foxglove, no. Blue witch nightshade, no. Hemlock, no. Oleander, no.

Evelyn every morning. Walk to the ridge. Eyes to the ground. Eyes up. Eyes to the ground. The grasses, the wild-growing flowers, she knows their names, each one, but she's opted while walking for all the days, this one and beyond, not to name them, not to think of them with specificity. Resist that. Grasses bent over. Not elegiac. Not adjective-laden to exist. Just grasses. Wind. Ocean. Every now and then moving in the water, a sea lion. Sea lions.

The cabin she shares with her son and daughter has windows made of the glass covers of old pinball machines. The sides are scrap wood girded inside with mud and felt. The outhouse is thirty paces from the front door. The roof is tin, and when it rains the three of them lie on the bed and close their eyes and listen. Life is so much lying down, getting up, lying down again. She can remember her son as a toddler, sick and wrapped in a cashmere scarf she'd gotten as a gift, her son lying on the window seat of the apartment she'd shared with her husband, sweating and then freezing and then sweating. She'd circled him with hot tea and chalky orange baby aspirin. Her worry then was a bag she dragged behind her always. She cannot muster it now. Used to be: next day, next day. Now: now.

When she walks from their cabin to the town,

encroachment is something she cannot help but think of. People in the town for a day or two days, a long weekend. They carry books with fresh bookmarks. They wear ponchos that have the appearance of being hand-knit but are likely bought from stores. They ogle the mist and laugh while eating nasturtiums off the vines. Like her life every day is the weekend life to which people aspire as a short term but then weekdays money, fluorescents, packaged meat. Ronald Reagan. She cannot not think of Ronald Reagan. His long cowboy-actor face. His swoop of shoe-polish hair. Near the Headlands, she comes upon flattened patches in the grass where some animal has spent the night, and she feels it her duty to lie down, too, to curl to the shape made there. Lie down.

The sky is a blend of blue and mist, and Evelyn has been all of these: Evelyn June Seven, Evie, Eve, Evelyn Masterson née Seven. Honey, Dear, Mommy, Mom, Seven, nothing. Evelyn June Seven wore pale blue almost exclusively and skated up and down the halls of her apartment building. Evie's father owned a seventy-five-seat movie theater several blocks from their house, and she stood in the back and ate red candy coins and waited for the moment when there was nothing but two faces close to each other on the screen. Eve drank beer from the bottle while listening to men play trumpet in a bar with peanut shells on the floor. She didn't need sleep. She didn't wear cardigans. Evelyn Masterson served shrimp scampi for ten at the table that had belonged to her in-laws. Honey crawled from her single bed to her husband's in the early morning when the new sun made a halo around the curtains. Dear made toast and tea to lay out on the Formica breakfast room table before the trains started taking suited men to newsstands and office buildings. Mommy was up in the night pulling at blankets and looking at the moon through windows. Mom was peripheral but needed when needed and not when not. Seven knew all the plants, plants more than people. Seven walked sometimes as if floating. Seven ate less each day. Seven made herself cloudlike with the clouds. She wanted less personness and more bird. Untether became her mantra. Untether. Lie down.

The last day is the last day they planned, to the letter. Foxglove and nightshade and oleander. The redwoods have a sheen of mist outside the fogged-over window of the communal kitchen. The plants root into each other under-ground in their secretive parley. She thinks she can hear it: their grasping, their bending. The people are all around the table. They have committed to talking little and if possible, not at all. There is the human noise of drinking, of the bodies. The children go quickly to sleep. She can remember lying in bed with her T. S. Eliot poems as a teenager ("till human voices wake us"), her monogrammed pen, a gift from her mother, in her left hand. She'd always found it special that she was left-handed. It meant something, she'd once convinced herself. Nothing meant something. The western bluebirds cackle in streaks and spin around a cloud of ravens. She sees the blue and the black out the window like the rippling ribbons of dancers in a caravan. Her moth-er's face lowers close to hers, the powdery cheeks, the matte red lips. How obvious that this is what comes to her: her mother. She disappoints herself. The ravens loop up above the treetops. The bluebirds are nowhere to be seen. Oh, for the bluebirds. Two hundred yards beyond the tree line, the ocean pulls up and over itself again. And we drown.

◆

The city, New York, Manhattan, is more than Hannah would have imagined, had she let herself imagine things beyond mushroom soup in hand-carved bowls (again), beyond maneuvering in the middle of the night to the outhouse with bare feet in the mud and pine needles (again), beyond shitty evenings in the communal kitchen where men with gray beards affixed to their chins like entire dangling opossums pushed their thighs into hers under the table (again).

She and her brother camped the whole way, west to east. In the desert, with wind and scorpions and motorcyclists; in the mountains, where they were ill equipped for the weather and moved from their makeshift tent into the truck, in a farm field, where they ate greens from someone's careful garden and slept with who knew how many cats in a barn full of gas cans and tractor parts, at the southern edge of Lake Erie in Geneva-on-the-Lake. It was not the most direct route, but the lake reminded them of their ocean, and a woman with red hair brought them to her beach rental and fed them flown-in crab legs with melted butter and marveled again and again that it was the first animal they'd ever eaten. No animals, but: mushrooms when she was seven that made her think her hands had turned into twin bears and her face was sequins, or standing in the stream for meditation at five A.M. in their underwear no matter what the temperature, or black beauties when she was ten that kept her awake for days. Everyone thought that was funny or at least helpful because she swept every single surface, even the outdoor paths between cabins. The waist-length braids. The white clothes on Wednesdays. The naked yoga at dusk when the sunlight was lifting itself away from the trees. The vats of plain, cheap fabric they hand-dyed and hung from lines between the pine trees. The endless goat-milk yogurt with bee honey on the woodstove and then in mason jars. The nights in the summer where they lay in the open-air central building in a hum of human arms and feet and heads as close as possible to the man they all called father who was not her father and only really father to some of the babies, but still.

And then: Times Square is a brilliant onslaught. *Coca-Cola, Midori Melon Liqueur, JVC, Taboo II Theater, The Harem, XXX.* Maybe she would be a city person. Cartoony paintings of women mainly unclothed drop down the sides of marquees, and Hannah can think only of the hot springs they hiked to every month, all of the women together and naked in the water, breasts weightless and bobbing at the water line, and all of their long braids partially submerged.

Her brother gawks at the buildings. He leans his head back until he might tip fully onto the sidewalk. She doesn't allow herself that. She walks purposefully. She looks straight ahead or at her feet. She tries not to think about the pink, hand-dyed/hand-sewn pants she's wearing with a black coat they'd found at a thrift store in Pennsylvania. She sits at a bench along the stone retaining wall surrounding Bryant Park as if she has done it every day. She won't give herself away.

People wear bright, patterned jackets, and they don't greet each other, they don't slow down to observe or wonder. The taxis and buses belch and lumber and zip. The only birds she sees are pigeons. Their necks flutter with ruffles of purple and green, and they launch up and around together in perfect spirals as if they rehearsed in alleyways to synchronize.

It will be easy to find their father. At least that is what
they think. Though she claimed she'd shed her past entirely
and along with it all of her sentimentality, their mother
had kept a gold-twined stack of monogrammed stationery
in a box under the bed: Evelyn Masterson, 25 Sutton Place,
No. 12.

Her brother buys two hot dogs for them with what's left
of their money. A man moves slowly by on crutches that
have been wrapped with rainbows of colored tape. Wom-
en in heavy makeup lean into each other and laugh. The
fur collars of their coats blend. Their faces are that close.
It starts to snow then, and she's never seen it before. The
flakes are just as she would have imagined had she let herself imagine things. If she didn't care what people thought,
she would open her palms in front of her body and watch
the snow melt on her hands.

They decide to leave the truck where it is parked, though
likely illegally, and walk to the building where her brother
lived as a small child. The sidewalks are papered with candy
wrappers and flattened blue-and-white coffee cups and
newspaper shards, and the snow is beginning to coat all of
it in its white film. In front of Grand Central, taxis honk
and idle. People are either rushing or standing and smoking.
As they pass St. Bart's, she lets herself stop and lean her
head back at the wonder of the dome and its tilework, the
order and pattern of which are nothing like the patchwork
cabin where she was raised. They walk past a huddle of
men sharing a bottle, and then there is the river and the
tan awl of the Queensboro Bridge, just as her brother has
described it. The building they enter is simple, a brick rectangle with a green awning over the door. If she'd let herself
imagine, she might have imagined something more ornate.

The doorman requires some talking to, but eventually he makes a call and lets them into the elevator.

The elevator opens directly into the apartment on the twelfth floor with its wide marble entry, and there is the man she presumes to be her father. He has more hair than she'd expected and no beard, and he wears a blue button-up shirt and has his arms extended out toward them. He is crying, so she wills herself to go to him.

She does not miss her mother yet. She doesn't allow herself that. She won't allow herself that until years later when she's lying in bed with some woman (again), when she's in that moment of after and waiting for something (again), and she sees her mother almost like a cloud above her, her braids now encased with vines and mud and so much longing. The great tragedy of Hannah's life will be this: she will hold herself back forever and for always. She'll laugh at parties. She'll mock her childhood. She'll live in seventeen different apartments in the city. She'll acquire bed sheets with people, shared pots and pans, strands of plug-in lights to wrap around window frames. She'll hold other faces in her two palms up close to her own face. But she will never be able to love.

She will go through all the motions, she will be so good at going through the motions, she will. The whole big world.

Dick Cheney Was Not My Father

But he could have been. My father was a similar man. And his name was Richard Cheney, though he never went by Dick, and he never lived at the Naval Observatory. Rather, he was an orthopedic surgeon in suburban Kansas City who said things like, "These hands are gold," to people at dinner parties where he was often the one who ate more than his fair share of the shrimp and dove into the pool drunk in his clothes because he thought everything he did was a fun spectacle.

In his seventies and still believing too much in his own infallibility, my father invested heavily in blockchain and Bitcoin, two things he knew nothing about, and lost almost all his money. After, he and my mother still lived in their house with an elaborate pool designed to look like a naturally-occurring jungle waterscape because they'd paid it off, and it was cheaper to stay, but they'd started eating dinner out at sad places with buffet lines, and their vacations no longer involved air travel, which is how my wife Selma and I found ourselves in a state park cabin next door to my parents' state park cabin in Mound City, Missouri, where over a million migrating birds, snow geese mainly, stopped off each year to preen and rest and yell at each other until taking off again. None of this was tragic.

("Who is Dick Cheney?" my son who is reading over my shoulder asks me now. He never knew my father who died the year he was born and knows of him only as "Your grandpa," and my son, seven now, certainly has no idea about *the* Dick Cheney, former Vice President, war criminal, and "really not a bad guy," according to my father. In my college composition class, we wrote an essay about "rugged individualism" and how the idea of the rugged individual is a particularly American and maybe a particularly male idea, as compared to collectivism found in some other countries, and it strikes me as I look at my son with his hair in braids and his pink sweatshirt that the kind of masculinity associated with the rugged individual is dying or maybe even dead in large swaths of America. Was I a Dick Cheney? No. Much to my father's dismay, I couldn't fix things or build things. I couldn't shoot a gun. I couldn't hold my own in a golf game. I couldn't slap other men on the back while we joked about taxes. I probably couldn't survive in a wilderness setting. Pussy, Patsy, Pansy, Nervous Nellie, these were all things my father had called me at one point or another, but somehow I'd never been able to hate him. "Dick Cheneys are rugged individuals," I tell my son, though it means nothing to him, and it's not a compliment, but it's not fully an insult either.)

In the morning in Mound City, Missouri, my wife Selma and I sit across from my mother and father and eat grits at a diner a few minutes down the road from the state park cabins, in the small stretch of the town where several antique stores all seem to sell the same racist yard ornaments.

"Your father has always wanted to see this, these birds," my mother says.

"News to me," my father says and adjusts his sweater, so it's pulled taut over his stomach. He'd never developed the pot belly of so many men his age. He grabs the remaining piece of bacon on my plate, which I wanted, but I don't stop him because this is our dynamic now. A few years ago, I might have pulled my plate an inch or two out of his reach to fuck with him, but now I want to let him have it, the bacon, the birds, whatever.

"Well, I mean, you expressed an interest," my mother says. She has finished her breakfast and is wiping her lipstick off on a cloth napkin before reapplying it, thick and brown-red, as she has done after every single meal of her adult life. This bird interest was something I didn't know about my father, and it seemed suspect. I could only remember him trying to aggressively trap the pigeons that nested in the eaves of the house I grew up in. Because it mattered to my dad, and even though I was better at weed and video games, I'd tried at things like BB guns and sports. A new one every season, though none of my friends played and instead spent after-school hours skateboarding around convenience stores to see who was best at stealing cigarettes. Junior year of high school, I stopped going to basketball practice and started breaking into the back entrances of movie theaters or taking mushrooms in abandoned buildings downtown, and when the coach called home, my father talked to me minimally for several weeks before one night gathering all the balls in the basement into a trash bag, footballs and basketballs and soccer balls and baseballs, slamming them into the trash can in the snow by the garage.

Next door to the diner where we have breakfast, there is a store for birders, with the expected bird books and feeders, but also baseball hats with stuffed animal goose heads sewn onto the fronts, and I buy those for all of us. This is maybe ostentatious when my dad was counting ones and coins to pay for the breakfast. Also, I'm sure the locals have had their share of bird tourists and don't find it as humorous as I do for the four of us to be walking through town honking and with those fabric stuffed goose heads bouncing out over our foreheads. My dad gets into it, and I can see for a minute the younger him, certain of purpose as he pushes his chest out and makes his arms into sharp angles, but my mom is embarrassed, and Selma, who is never embarrassed by anything, is honking more than anyone and flapping her arms like wings.

Here I am, forty and childless with my mother holding her breath, hoping my wife, Selma, thirty-five, will bring forth something to distract my mother and father from this fast forward of their current life.

I was one of those people, like so many people I knew, who didn't have any absolutist sense of trajectory and what should be next. The things people my age knew seemed unessential and thin: how to play board games at big tables with friends while drinking whiskey and how to hibernate for days while binge watching almost anything; most of the rest of the life stuff, the grown-up stuff, we still somehow didn't know.

◆

Unbeknownst to my father, I'd invested a few years before in a capsule supplement that relied on pyramid-style distribution and targeted yoga moms who drank cold-pressed juices and shared keto recipes on Instagram and gently shamed each other with selfies displaying their health and wellness, particularly immediately post child-birth. A friend from college owned the company, and my investment turned out well. I'd made a lot of money in a fairly short time, and I had random bottles of the stuff all over my apartment. Sometimes, Selma and I shook them like maracas while we cooked or watched movies. I'd been a fuckup for more than a decade, withdrawing from col-lege classes, getting fired from one and then the next bar-tending job, trying and failing at a couple of corporate sales jobs, ending up working for hourly pay at a place that sold sports gear at a mall close to my house. It was dumb luck that the supplement thing had worked, and I felt guilty about it, about the fact that these supplements did nothing more than, say, eating an extra carrot in the morning, but the people who took them swore by them. I would have told dinner party shrimp Richard Cheney about this windfall, but it was impossible to tell buffet Richard Cheney; doing so seemed cruel.

("So, you used to be kind of a fuck-up?" my son says. "Don't say fuck-up," I say, but I laugh. And then, "Yes, kind of. Well, more than kind of." In the years of my son's childhood, I was the level of well-off where I could book an international flight and not think too much about it. I could go to a grocery store that specialized in food from other coun-tries and buy ten different cheeses and as many boxes of

European crackers and a plastic container of all the types
of olives for a party Selma and I were having, and I wouldn't
have to look at the prices of any of it. My son had all the
sneakers he wanted. There was something in capitalism,
some baked-in feeling that maybe men especially needed
to have that kind of money to be loose and easy in the
world. If I said that out loud to Selma, she'd be appalled
by the sexism, and she would be right; it was sexist. Still,
with this kind of money, I felt stronger and better and
more virile in ways that often made me feel disgusted
with myself. "You should," I said to my son, who was putting minifigures into some kind of elaborate diorama
he'd built of leaves and stones on the windowsill, "move
to the middle of nowhere and learn agribusiness. No, not
agribusiness, plain old agriculture. Eat carrots you pull
from the ground without washing them." "You're losing it,
Dad," he said, and probably he was right. "No, really," he
said, and now he looked a little worried, "do you think we
need to be farmers? I heard you say to Mom it's the end
of the world." He was old enough to understand hyper-
bole, to know I didn't mean it literally. Still, having grown
up hearing phrases like this, I'm sure his generation was
carting peripheral panic everywhere they went. "No, no,
we're fine. We don't need to be farmers. We're okay," I said
to him, and his forehead smoothed, and he went back to
trying to click a plastic sword into the c-shaped hand of a
knight the size of his pinky.)

We get in my dad's car in front of the bird store. Instead
of putting the key into the ignition, he puts the key into
the heating vent up and to the right from the ignition and
Selma and I, still laughing from all the goose imitation,

laugh like this is the joke we think it is, but then he pulls
the key out of the heating vent with its plastic slats and
puts it in again, and my mom moves his hand over to the
ignition without saying a word. We are all quiet in the
car, and I focus on the question of why my dad still has
a car that starts with an actual key instead of a button.
In the rear-view mirror, I can see my dad's face tense. My
mom turns on some AM station where a woman is berating
another woman for caring about a man too much and in
the wrong way. My parents graduated high school in the
late 1950s in a cloud of suburban positivity that extended
to white people in their teens and 20s. They could do anything. They were too old to be hippies and too young to
have been affected very much by WWII. They were in this
soft pocket that delivered them forward with an inno-
cence not well-suited to aging and disease and the actual
fucking world.

The radio woman yells at the other woman, and somehow
this antagonism that's entirely apart from him lulls my
dad. I look at the mirror again, and the skin on his forehead
softens and evens out, and he starts the car, and then we
are driving down a two-lane road that goes from pavement
to gravel as if we are actually going back in time. We pass
farm fields and houses that have decayed beyond the point
of no return. A boy with a pellet gun is shooting into the
side of a shed, and the ping ping ping is a dull rattle rhythm
and then gone.

"So, a million snow geese. Should be quite a sight," my
mother says, and taps her nails on the dash and crosses
and re-crosses her legs. The car is the same car they've had
forever, a very old Mercedes automatic that I once forgot
to put into gear, and it rolled down the driveway and into

the yard across the street where it crushed our neighbor's highly cultivated perennial garden, and my dad, who I'd thought would call me a waste of space or drag me over to the torn-up garden to belittle me in front of the neighbor, had instead taken me aside at the top of the driveway and said, "Edward Samuels, that pretentious fuck with all his flowers labeled with Latin name tags. Take that." The next day, he'd sent Samuels a check for the work it would take to recreate the garden, and we'd never talked about it again. It was maybe the closest we'd ever been.

Snow geese are generally white, but some of them are blue, so within a group of snow geese, you might see a hundred white heads and a few blue-feathered bodies, and the babies are shockingly self-sufficient and can leave the nest a few hours after coming out of an egg. And that is the extent of my snow goose knowledge gleaned from Selma reading aloud from an Audubon entry off her phone in the car, but I do envy the immediate lurch from infancy to action, and I wonder if the years humans spend with parents infantilize them forever.

The approach to the preserve is shielded by trees, so there is the chaos of noise before we see anything. Then there they are, birds so tight together they form bird clouds, and the sound as we approach is an extravagant, relentless honking. The lake ahead, which during other months must be an expanse of blue water, is entirely punctuated with the white feathered bodies. In other words: close up, a million is a lot of birds.

"Should we stop here?" Selma says, gesturing toward a spot where there are a few picnic tables. The air in the car has gotten overheated. Selma is sweating in her goose hat and down coat.

I crack the window and say, "Dad, should we pull over?" But my father guns it instead. He speeds forward, and birds ascend in a swoosh and a clatter, a wide wake all around us. The road ends, but my father keeps driving, farther and faster.

I open my mouth to say something, but my mother looks back at me with a look that says no, absolutely not, and Selma grabs my hand. I see my parents flying, wings instead of forearms, the sky a solid thing that pushes them toward more sky, toward beyond and stratosphere and whatever ever after we all secretly want to believe in but can't and don't. The car accelerates, and I swear the wheels leave the ground. I intake breath, and we are a few inches up. The geese are beating clouds of white and feather, and we are some kind of hovercraft or car balloon or argument against gravity, and weight is nothing. Age and time are nothing.

My dad dies that year in early summer of an undiscovered subdural hematoma after a fall on the patio about which he tells no one but my mother, and maybe there will be a heaven, even though none of us believed in it with any of the required vim or really at all, there it will be, and maybe Dick Cheney will encounter Richard Cheney, and there will be food of course because it's heaven and the kind of place where simply imagining the creamsicles of your childhood will bring them to your hands and the pale orange ice cream is imbued with summer and the breath-holding happy of being up late in the yard where fireflies make ziplines around the night, or if you're Dick Cheney, you imagine a whole side of beef roasted over an outside fire the size of a suburban bathroom, or if you're my Dick Cheney, Richard, it's golf course hamburgers and the afternoon goes on forever with no threat of evening, and maybe Dick Cheney meets Richard Cheney beside a body of water where the temperature is so good you don't even have to think about temperature, and the birds are gentle songbirds that flit more than flap, and they both have such ease that I want to hold it against them, but then maybe not; maybe I won't, because really we all deserve peace, don't we?

(No, we don't really levitate in the car with my parents and the birds. But it feels that way. It feels like we are floating. It feels like the world gives us that. Selma is pregnant and it's a bean or a button, and nobody, not even us knows, but my dad will be dead soon. Any attempts to overlay meaning on any of it fail. All I can say is: secrets are everywhere. Pain is, too.

I'll tell this story to my son, as if we were really flying, "We were in the car," I'll say, "Your grandpa was driving, so fast. And then it was like we were flying with all those birds," I'll say, when he can't sleep and it's two A.M. and he needs something fanciful to distract him from the night. Fatherhood had focused me in a way no one, especially me, would have anticipated. Really, I was the best father, and it's maybe the only thing I've ever been or ever would be good at, but I knew it was enough.

In the story I tell my son, the geese are in their Vs, hundreds, thousands, a million, all of them going somewhere, and the world is winged beauty, a pulse, an idea, a sequined ever-moving sigh. My dad is gone. I am still here. The sky. Well, the sky is the sky.)

Ghosts

People will say Ry must have planned the robbery for weeks. They'll want purpose and emotion and strategy. They'll say she had a gun tucked into a pocket. They'll say she must have been desperate: four kids at home or a dying parent in need of a kidney.

None of that was true. The fact was, Ry was not rich, but she'd paid rent. She worked in a place on campus where sorority girls bought bubble tea. She had no dependents, a decent supply of microwavable Indian food, and several kinds of cereal.

The bank teller was an older man with precise hair who wore a mask printed with golden apples. Before she passed him the note she'd scrawled on a receipt in the bank parking lot, he said, "Oh, honey, how can I help you?" When she handed him the note, his look was more shock than fear, as in, *Really? You?* She left with her pink bag stuffed full of cash.

It surprised no one more than her.

◆

Hayes and Solace walk to school like this every day, up the hill of 9th Street, left to the flat school building with its many eyebrow windows, someone's dream of innovation in the 1960s. The campanile bells ring from campus a few blocks away, and it makes them feel like they are in a movie from another time, something with love and war.

"I would not be in love in a movie," Hayes says to Solace on a Tuesday when they meet in front of their apartment building. The fall leaves have been on the ground long enough they crackle, but it's not very cold. They both wear hoodies. Hayes's solid gray and Solace's airbrushed with an ice cream cone on the front and yellow fluorescent "Be Cool" underneath.

"What do you mean?" Solace says. He is almost ten and loves press-on nails and musicals. He hates the bottoms of lakes and apartment carpeting.

A car races by, too close to the curb, and he steps back and adjusts his backpack, which has many small stuffed animals hanging from the zipper like tiny safari trophies.

"What I mean," Hayes says, "is I wouldn't want to be the person in love in the movie. I'd rather be the other person, the one who gives the person in love advice." Hayes is ten and loves black holes and communism. He admires atheism and hates gummy fruit snacks.

"I could be the person in love then," Solace says.

Hayes lives with his dad who is the produce manager at the co-op. Their refrigerator is full of unwanted disfigured fruits and vegetables. His mom is gone, but she sometimes sends Polaroids of the mountains that Hayes hangs from metal clothespins in his room, a converted walk-in closet where he's strung lines of LED lights and super glued stuffed animals onto one whole wall so he can, when he's upset or angry or simply wants to, run himself from the floor mattress into the plush wall and feel nothing but softness and joy.

Solace's mom works in the communications office of the hospital, so he spends school conference days walking up and down the stairs in the hospital atrium where people sit at tables, sad about someone dying or happy about someone being born. His room shares its back wall with Hayes's room and has a peachy ceiling and pale green walls and several of the paper lanterns he thinks people who live in cities, people he wants to be, sit under while eating on the back terraces of well-reviewed restaurants.

Sometimes at night, when their parents have taken and plugged in their phones, Hayes and Solace knock on their shared wall. One knock is *I can't sleep.* Two knocks is *I can't either.* Three knocks is *goodnight* or *tomorrow* or *wait.* Four knocks is *I hate everyone but you.*

Halfway up the hill to school, they stop at the construction site. It's walled off by chain-link fencing and speckled with excavators and telehandlers ready to tear down a building that was once home to a film company that made low-budget horror films (per Hayes's dad), and it was, "a shame for it to go" (per Solace's mom), but, she said, "communities can't always afford to prop up every old thing."

"I think when they tear it down tomorrow, it's going to release a bunch of old-movie ghosts," Solace says. His forehead is crisscrossed from leaning into the fence. He doesn't know his dad, and his mom never talks about him, so he thinks of him as people in commercials about detergent or sports drinks or a kind of blurry dad ghost who could be anyone at all.

"You don't really believe in that shit," Hayes says and lets his backpack hang down on his forearms.

"You're right, I don't," Solace says, even though he's not sure, and they keep walking.

A block away from the bank, Ry stuffs her face mask and hat into the bag in one of the alleys between the bank and campus. She stacks the money on the back of a toilet in a bathroom in the student union and thinks, *it doesn't look like much*, but, also, it's more money in one spot than she's ever seen. She switches her bag, a cloth reversible bag, from the pink tie-dyed side to the light-blue-with-flowers side and leaves the bathroom. People sit around a table in the common space and play chess.

Someone in glasses, someone she probably would like if she saw him at the bar where her sister works, shouts, "Man, you're playing chess *old school*," as in, Ry assumes, not on an iPad or a phone. The chess pieces are pink and, though they are probably plastic, they look like rose quartz, the kind she learned about in a middle school geology class when you could find yourself excited about pretty stones.

She and her sister had binged the show about the beautiful woman chess champion. Her sister had shown up at Ry's apartment with an Instapot full of chicken mole, and they watched in one bleary overnight stretch.

"Of fucking course," her sister had said, "It makes it so boring, her beauty. Give me an average-looking woman chess player trouncing everyone and still getting their admiration. That, I'd like to watch."

Ry had agreed, but also, she wanted to be the beautiful chess player.

"You have good tits, at least," her sister said and threw her paper plate, now soaked in what looked like dried blood, into the trash can.

Ry had stepped out on the rectangle of concrete outside her sliding glass door where the morning light was coming in behind the trees, pink in strips. Maybe it wasn't beauty she wanted, exactly, but expectant faces in a room, possibility.

Hayes's and Solace's teacher has shelves of Pokémon plushies near the reading rug where they sit on a Tuesday, each of them only about twenty pages into the same assigned book about a dog and a tollbooth.

"It's kind of embarrassing," Hayes says to Solace when they get up at break and wait in line at the fountain, over which you'd once been able to lean, but now where you fill bottles to drink later when you are seated far enough apart from other people. The plushies teacher makes a hand motion near his face while making his eyes look smiley, and the motion means, *Hayes, pull your mask up,* so he does.

"What do you mean?" Solace says to Hayes.

"I mean, the striving," Hayes says as they walk down the linoleum that is mainly gray but has periodic squares in bright colors. Hayes's dad talked a lot about *striving*, about *the trap of capitalism,* about how it made you hate yourself enough to buy more and then spin there forever, hating, wanting, buying, again.

"I mean thinking having those plushies makes us like him, *that* striving."

"But people have to try," Solace says, "Right? They shouldn't just not try?"

Someone runs into Solace near the doors to the playground and says nothing, not *I'm sorry,* not *my bad,* not *oops.* This is something Solace's mom has prepared him for, and he knows already how to pretend and ignore. Hayes speed walks ahead, trips the person, and then backs up so he won't be found out.

"I didn't need that," Solace says.

"I know," Hayes says. "Still."

They walk out to recess where all they ever do is swing: higher, legs working, higher, jump, start again.

Outside the student union, away from the chess players, Ry braids her long hair into two braids while she walks. Several girls in big sweatpants and midriff shirts walk by her laughing at something. Their teeth are as white as miniature marshmallows.

Ry hadn't gone to college. She started working at the makeup counter at Kohl's during high school, and then she'd gotten the bubble tea job. Her sister, who was older by three years, went to college for a semester and then quit to work at the sports bar where Ry spent too much time playing Pac-Man and drinking whatever drinks her sister was willing to give her. At first, she thought the Pac-Man ghosts were all the same, the same level of aggressive, the same randomness, the same chase. She learned over time, though, they each had their own personality, their own game and method. The red one was relentless. The pink one was sneaky. The blue one wasn't on its own as much of an aggressor but could team up with the red one. The orange one was a scaredy-cat. Ry's mom had said this to her when she was younger, "Don't be a scaredy-cat," when they walked through their neighborhood at night. She had been, though. Every noise, every car, every person. The thing was, though the ghosts had powers, they were still ghosts: fleeting, there and then gone.

"I want to be the red ghost," Ry had said to her sister the

previous Saturday, even though she never had been a red-ghost type.

"Sorry, girl, you're not the red ghost," her sister told her. She held two soapy pint glasses in each hand so four total and, somehow, she broke none of them. "You're the blue one, like you're not going to, you know, initiate, but if red is into it, you're down."

On the way home from school, Hayes convinces Solace to fit through the gap in the chain-link fence at the back of the lot where the old movie building is prepped for demolition. The building is taped off, but no one is there, and the construction vehicles are dormant, so for a few minutes they sit down on the step at the back of the building.

"We should go in," Hayes says.

"Let's just sit," Solace says and messes with the lid of his water bottle. "Did you know the military is experimenting with electromagnetic forcefields to play with gravity so some day we could live on the moon if they figure it out?"

"Weird. There's a hawk on that pole," Hayes says, "or is it an eagle?"

"Hawk. The head isn't white, and eagles don't usually come this far from a water source."

"Oh, okay. And I would not want to go to the moon unless space travel changes completely."

Hayes gets up, tries the door, and finds it unlocked. "Come on," he says to Solace. Hayes goes first, and Solace grabs Hayes's forearm. It's dark, but chutes of light come through the upper windows, which are planted at the tops of walls like the windows at their school. They go into separate rooms with shared walls and knock on them the way they do at home. Hayes is both scared and exhilarated alone in a semi-dark room with filing cabinets, and Solace is nervous in another room with shiny beanbag chairs.

They meet back in the hallway, where empty beer cans are lined up like an art installation.

The girl with the braids surprises them. She's sitting on the floor at the end of the dark hall where they have been walking.

She says, "Hey, don't be afraid of me. I'm not scary. I'm fine," even though they didn't ask, and then, "I didn't have a weapon, but they thought I had a weapon, so it was weirdly the same as having one."

"We don't even know you," Hayes says to her.

"Come on," she says to them.

"Come where?" Solace says, "And why?" His nails are painted pale blue, imprecisely applied. The polish makes his fingers look like bits of sky.

"Why do we do anything we do, is what I'm wondering," the girl says. She snaps at two hair bands around her wrist. It looks breakable in the way of a birdwing. "Don't mistake me for fragile," she says while looking at the ceiling. Though it's a strange thing to say out loud, they both know exactly what she means.

Ry walks them into a room and picks up a long metal canister, the kind that maybe held a roll-down map from another decade, and swings it at one of the glass plates separating door and wall. What is she thinking of then? Of her sister sad on a Monday. Of a stranger naked on her bed and looking up at her bare stomach. Coming into the bathroom to see her mother, curled over on herself like a reptile, cutting her toenails into the bathtub. Life is a series of knitted-together indecencies maybe. Maybe the real work is to loosen oneself from them every now and then. She doesn't know. Maybe that's the thing: to not know and keep going the way people walk through the dark of a haunted house and scream sometimes with delight at the surprises.

"Whoa," the boy in the plain hoodie says. The other boy, the one in the ice cream cone hoodie, makes his eyes big as the glass falls into pieces on the old carpeting. He stands with toes turned out, arms at his sides light as willow branches.

"What? They're going to demolish this whole place tomorrow, so, you know, why not?" She motions to them with her hands and arms, as in, *Come on* and *join me.*

The gray hoodie boy pulls on the built-in wooden shelf, and it disconnects from the wall easily. The bookshelves, the wood, everything in the building, come from the time Ry's mom romanticizes, the land of her mom riding her old bike in the country for hours and even through swarms of butterflies landing on her mom's hands and forehead, or so she has told Ry and her sister more than once. Butterflies have never landed on Ry, though once when she sat in the green space behind her apartment, three triangulating grasshoppers stared at her, an inch from her ankle, and she thought, at the time, it meant something.

The boy holds the shelf like a baseball bat and looks around for something to strike. He makes eye contact with the other boy and then sets the board down the way someone would relocate a snail to get it out of the line of pedestrian traffic: soft, gentle.

"I don't think I'm as interested in destruction as I thought I'd be," he says.

Ry says, "Yeah, you know what, same here, agreed. Are you hungry? What about cereal? I have a lot of cereal."

"We both like cereal," the gray hoodie boy says without even looking at the other boy.

Cereal is its own through-line, and Ry can follow it from dry cereal on a high-chair tray in a warm some-thing-cooking kitchen where her mother danced to '80s metal, then to cereal in front of a Saturday TV while her sister jumped next to her on the couch, then to cereal alone in her apartment bed looking out the window at midnight and swearing the tree shadows were people, and the crickets were chanting something like: *take me, take me.*

Hayes and Solace follow the girl out of the building. It's darker now because it's the time of year when the night starts to take over early and quickly. Hayes and Solace aren't usually out without parents at this time, so there's a thrill to it. They both have phones, but their ringers are still off from having them silenced at school, and they aren't old enough or at least not the kind of kids to have them forever in their hands. Rather, they are buried in backpacks beneath mechanical pencils and Starburst wrappers.

The girl leads them across the street at the light at 9th and Emery and then down the hill toward the farthest building, the one that abuts the woods and is three build-ings back from the one where Solace and Hayes live in their adjacent apartments.

"Do you live here, too?" Hayes says. He looks back at the woods, which are dark now and could contain anything.

"I do," the girl says. "Do you?"

"Yep," Hayes says. "We both do." But then he has a small feeling like a splinter and wonders if he should be reveal-ing this information to this person whose apartment he is entering from the back sliding-glass door. He should have stopped at his own apartment. He should have gone inside and gotten a damaged apple from the refrigerator and locked the front door and waited for his dad to get home so they could watch *Cosmos* while eating a discounted margherita frozen pizza.

The girl opens a cabinet and pulls out a box of cereal whose cardboard top is ripped. Her bowls are plastic and in bright colors. She fills three of them with cereal and almond milk, and they go to the couch and sit cross-legged in a triangle.

She sets her bowl down on the coffee table for a second, pulls her bag from where it sits on the floor, and spreads money over the table the way Hayes has seen people doing in movies.

"Holy shit," Hayes says.

Solace says, "That's a lot of money. What are you going to do with it? Buy a Tesla?"

"Ha, no. It's not enough for a Tesla," she says and laughs. "You can each have some." She hands them some of the money. "Take it," she says. "Really." And they look at each other and then put it into their backpacks.

Teslas make Hayes sad. With their lift-up doors, they seem like an old person's fantasy of the future.

The girl's phone is buzzing.

"You should check that," Hayes says. "It's been going crazy for a while now. Maybe someone needs you." Hayes and Solace both envision their parents standing together in one of their two kitchens, worrying.

The girl opens the sliding door. The room floods with night noises. Somewhere, owls are tormenting a chicken, with all the corresponding hooting and then squawking.

The bird noise builds, a back and forth, cacophony, and then silence.

Hayes's eyes go to the open back door. He thinks of the building ghosts waiting in the building. Maybe one of them is his mom, a ghost to him now, filmy, a series of pressed-together memories.

"Is no one going to say anything about the dead chicken?" Solace says.

Who knows, maybe it's minutes before the door to the apartment rumbles with knocking. There are cameras everywhere now, and police can solve crimes surprisingly quickly.

Ry gathers the money from the table back into the bag. She shoves protein bars into the pocket and fills a few plastic water bottles.

"Come on," she says to them. The ice cream hoodie boy hesitates. He sticks to the couch, but the gray hoodie boy pulls at him. They walk out the sliding door and into the woods where their shoes snap twigs, where they hold hands as a balm against the owls who are somewhere nearby gleefully tearing apart a dead chicken.

Ry closes her eyes in the dark. The lights of passing cars cast through the woods. The word *fractals* pops into her head. To her mind comes the phrase, "infinitely complex patterns repeating," something from a high school science class, back at a time when every day someone talked to her about fantastic facts and ideas and the future.

Pac-Man ghosts are encoded with a set number of options. Alive, alive, dot dot dot, forward, forward, dot dot dot, disappear.

In some other version of things, the two boys and the girl disappear in a puff of movie ghosts and Pac-Man ghosts, and still-live chickens, and unscary woods. They eat candy by a waterfall. Sleep comes easily. Nonpredatory mountain lions wander by. The stars are brighter than they've ever seen them. They miss no one. Of course, this isn't that world.

In this version, she sends them home. She goes home herself and puts the backpack in her closet under a pile of clothes. In the morning, she sits with cereal by her windows and sees the boys walking up the hill and turns her head. She puts on bright red lipstick and goes to stand behind a counter and serve bubble tea to sorority girls who've been trained into the kind of hyper politeness that makes her feel terrible about all the things she is and is not.

After work, she sits at the bar and talks to her sister and then watches while her sister flirts with two basketball players. She read a poem in high school about having to prepare a face for all the faces you'll meet, and her sister does it so well.

No one comes for her. She will wait for years. She'll marry someone average, live in an average one-story house on an average street with her average children. Sunsets might be out of the ordinary a few nights each fall, sometimes the orange of a cut-open peach. One year, the lilacs at the edge of her property will be so profuse and heady that sitting by them with her eyes closed in the morning will feel like swimming in thick purple water. She'll think so many times of saying to her children, "Once I robbed a bank," to get them to really look at her.

While she is at work, the day after the robbery, the excavators come and tear down the building. Nothing ghost-like emerges. No, that's not true. The handprints on film canisters balloon into dust clouds of past wants and old sadnesses. Red lips float up. Open mouths. Hands open.

Hands grasping. Most people miss it, though, this fog assemblage of things that once were but are no longer. Most people are driving, windows closed, listening to news of a war somewhere or a song whose words they know most of but not all.

By six P.M., when the traffic is heavy, when Hayes and Solace are home and knocking on their shared wall, all the things that made the building, the glass they didn't hit, the blue-taped shelves, the metal disks that held someone's beautifully scary movies, are rubble, are completely gone. *Take me, take me, take me,* the crickets say.

Our Female Geniuses

At the school auction, after drinks, after dinner, but before the program begins, the grownups huddle close to the stage. They are giddy. Their whitened teeth flash. Bare upper arms flex. Suit coats hang on the backs of chairs.

The scholarship girls line up on the stage, nervous but annoyed. One of them messes with her bangs, fluffing them up and then flattening them down. Another slips out of one shoe and then back in. Arms brush arms.

"Am I wrong or is it a particularly good class this year?" one man says to a woman, maybe his wife.

"You're not wrong," she says, and it begins.

Two women lean, facing out, against the stucco railing. The music stops inside, but they don't go in. Instead, they watch two people on the dark lawn.

"It wouldn't be a school auction without two people not married to each other fucking outside in darkness," one of the women on the balcony says. She's in a tight green satin dress with a row of meticulous fabric buttons going all the way up the side of her neck.

A waiter brings a tray out to the balcony, passes each of them a drink, and goes back in. The drinks are pale yellow with veined, edible flowers floating in them. The woman in the green dress pulls the flower from her drink and tosses it over the railing. It's their fourth hour of drinking.

"Ha. Let's hope it's not one of our husbands," her friend says. She's in white silk, loose and cowled at the neck, no sleeves, her black hair gathered at the back in rhinestone clips, or maybe they are actual diamonds.

"I don't know," green satin says. "I'm at the not-caring point. Take him, fine by me." She swallows the rest of her drink and sets the empty glass on the railing.

They are sharing a cigarette. It glows between them. In fact, their husbands are inside the double doors by a table where a card jutting out of a basket touts a trip to wine country: "Napa like you've never done Napa."

Outside, by the tree, the two people on the lawn aren't fucking, but they were. Now they are talking about how much they want each other, always want each other. He, the man by the tree, is the anchor on a television news show, and she, the woman, is a writer. An outsider might say, "Of course you want each other. You aren't married." To which they would insist, "No, it's not that. It's really not that." Or, actually, the man might say that. The woman, the writer, she might say the stage makeup on his shirt collars makes her cringe. She might say the texting for weeks before the sex was hotter than the actual sex. Still, she keeps at it. She doesn't want to let it go. She is divorced, and, when married, never did anything like fuck against a tree. What would have happened if they'd taken their own spouses to back yards and fucked against trees? If they'd sent tit pics or dick pics instead of things like, "Salmon tonight?"

"There should be two parallel track lives," green dress says. "Like how everyone always says, 'You only get one life,' but, really, you should get two."

"How do you mean?" white dress says.

"Like, you should have the one life you're living, the marriage, the kids, the job. You're good. You do what you're supposed to do. And then there's the other life, where you get to detach for maybe a weekend every month and do anything you want."

"Oh, I'd totally go for that. Work out whatever urges or demons or whatever. Go run a marathon or fuck a stranger or sit in the woods alone with no one saying something like, 'Can you get me some pretzels? I really don't feel like getting up right now,' as if, you know, I do."

The woman in the white dress finishes her drink and sets her glass next to the other empty glass on the railing. The glasses are the kind that look like saucers set on stems, and they glow in the lights under the balcony like they might lift off.

Inside, there's a drumroll and then some applause. The announcer starts talking again, and the crowd gets quiet.

Both women spent forever getting ready: Himalayan salt bath, under-eye patches, serums, (neck, forehead, chest, feet, ass), leave-in conditioner, toenails, cuticles, eyebrows, lashes, concealer, contour, highlight, setting spray, gloss. Now, it is all a bit askew, like in one of those photos where something is off, a car door handle on the hood of a car, but you have to spend a few minutes looking to find it.

An animal darts across the lawn and down the pea-gravel path and out of sight.

"Holy shit," green dress says. "Did you see that?"

"Was that a fucking fox?"

"We should go catch it, make it a pet."

"I can't tell if you're kidding. I think you're kidding."

"I'm kidding. Imagine me showing up at home dangling a fox from its tail like, 'Hey kids, look, a friend.'"

They both laugh, and white dress lights another cigarette. "Maybe we should all publicly smoke again. Does it really matter?"

"It doesn't. It doesn't matter at all. In ten years, when we are gasping for air because it's too hot to breathe or whatever, I'm going to call you and say, 'We should have been smoking all day every day. We should have been the ones fucking on the lawn. We shouldn't have waited for some parallel life.'"

The two of them lean over the balcony to see if they can, again, spot the fox.

The woman out by the trees, the writer, tells the man, the TV news personality, "My daughter is here."

The woman calls herself a writer, but really, she works for a nonprofit, so her writing is pamphlets and press releases. She also wrote stories sometimes, and sometimes she published them in small magazines that most of America knew nothing about. So, every now and then, she'd announce to her daughters, "I have a new story out," and her older daughter would look at her with what the writer knew was sympathy or maybe even antipathy when the writer told her the name of the journal.

The cars and buses whoosh beyond the stone walls around the grounds, which have boxwood hedges and

gravel paths and trees with engraved name plates announc-
ing tree names and dates of planting.

He says, "Which daughter? I assume the older one?"

"The older one, the difficult one, however you want to
categorize her."

In truth, her older daughter is not that difficult, at least
not in the way the writer herself was when she was seventeen. Sometimes she hears her leaving the apartment in
the middle of the night, but she doesn't intervene because
there is no evidence of anything alarming, no drugged eyes,
no drop in grades, no cuts on her thighs. But her daughter
is cruel and quiet and often, after entirely silent hours on
a Saturday might say something like, "You think that dress
makes you look good, don't you?"

"Usually, the middle or younger are difficult, right, rule
breakers? My youngest son is a nightmare."

"That's not the most helpful information," she says, but
she also grabs the front of his pants, where he is still hard
or hard again.

She looks up and sees an animal huddled at the concrete
base of the fountain. It's silvery, and she thinks it's a fox,
though it's not the bright-orange, white-tipped-tail fox
of childhood books. Once, when she was hiking with her
sister, an animal followed them down the path, not menacing but more scampering, almost like it wanted to play.
Still, they ran from it, screaming, and once they finally
ditched it, they disagreed about whether it was a fox or
a coyote. "Either way," her sister said, "it's a sign of something," but the woman, the writer, she knew nothing was
a sign of anything.

The animal by the fountain, whatever it is, is har-
ried-seeming, and she doesn't want to move because she

doesn't want to disturb it, but also, she's moving her hand and pushing the man back into the tree and hoping the bark rips the back of his shirt because she's tired of all this hiding.

"So, what is your daughter's talent, remind me?" the man asks, though it's weird to be asking right then, but they've been at this for several months, and they're accustomed to moving between things, personal, superficial, physical, in a way that feels seamless.

"Chess. That's her thing."

At the request of the school's administration, the scholarship girls did this at the auction each year: took coats, mingled, performed whatever they were particularly talented at, looked appealing.

"Ah, inspiring donations, of course," he says, but he's also moaning, or it's more guttural, more like a grunt, and then he comes in her hand, and some of it drips onto her dress, a tiny meteor of liquid on black. She leans down to wipe her hand in the grass.

"I love that you're so natural," he says, "that you don't try too hard like all these other women, the fake tits, the immobilized forehead, so much makeup. Fuck, I feel like I need to hose my wife down to see her actual face." He zips his pants and tucks in his shirt tightly in front, smooths it with both hands.

The woman had tried, though. She spent a long time, longer than she normally did, with her makeup, but her hair was everywhere, frizzing out. She stood in front of the hall mirror too long before leaving, and her older daughter, waiting in a floral dress that looked very nineteenth century said, "Ooh, maybe you'll get lucky, Mom. Maybe someone will grab your tits," and the writer tried to laugh as she walked down the stairs, out the door, and into a waiting car while the night gathered itself up, moved from gray-blue to navy, decided what kind of night to be.

"We probably shouldn't do this anymore," the newsman says. "Too many close calls."

The woman has been ready for a statement like this for weeks, and she is good at freezing herself completely when something she doesn't like flies toward her. If it hits her, she won't even feel it.

The woman hears drums and then applause casting out over the lawn.

"Sounds good," she says and straightens her dress and wipes at the stain with her fingertips. She looks up by the fountain, and the fox or coyote is gone.

Earlier, inside, the woman's daughter sat at a table with a chess board. She was on a velvet backless cube of a chair, and her dress draped down around the triangle of her legs. She sat forward at the edge of the cube, waiting. Her friend stood by the bar with her violin. She was supposed to play for people when they walked up and asked. The girl and her friend rolled their eyes at each other, and the friend put her bow and violin in one hand and did the beating-off gesture with her free hand. The friend laughed, and then an old-seeming couple approached the friend, and she started playing her violin for them while they nodded too much and smiled.

A waiter walked toward the girl and handed her what looked like a coke.

"I gave you something extra," the waiter said. He was probably only a couple of years older than she was. She didn't like to drink, hated the brain blurriness of it, but she humored him because he stood there too long, waiting for her to try it.

"Thanks, it's good," she said and looked down at the marble chess board with its carved pieces. Practically every girl she knew was long-haired, thin, and troubled, and there she was also being long-haired, thin, and troubled.

She messed with her hair, which was tawny almost like deer fur and never fully kempt. "Just you wait," was a thing that adults liked to say to her. "People aren't going to be able to keep their hands off you." No thanks, she always thought when people said that, but she never said it out loud. It was embarrassing to her how grownups, like young children, couldn't keep their hands off things. While she was playing for one old man earlier in the evening, another old man stood next to her and kept his hand on her shoulder for half the game, and no amount of shrugging and repositioning herself worked to shake him. She'd read a book for school where the male protagonist wanted a mute and attractive woman, and it had made her mad at herself that she was naturally a quiet person, that she was, without wanting to, fulfilling some aspect of this male fantasy. She'd then spent two weeks at school trying to change herself, to sit in the front row, to be the first one at the lunch table to start talking, to yell in the halls. But it hadn't worked, and soon she'd retreated to her normal self: thinking cutting things in her head but saying very few of them out loud. And, she'd noticed, it was like this that boys wanted her, even better if she said dark things about sex quietly, almost under her breath, or alluded to some emotional dysfunction. Smart but with a tiny, pretty glitch in the system.

◆

The woman in the green dress has turned so she's leaning her back against the balcony railing, and she's undone the few buttons at the top of the dress, so a bent triangle of the green satin flaps forward like a tongue.

At the last school event, the holiday party, she'd been with the newsman. He was always with someone. He fucked badly, quickly, and had come all over her shin in the pantry of a Maryland country club where head-sized jars of cocktail onions were right at eye level. After that night, she stopped responding to his messages and spent January chiding herself for being so susceptible.

"My elbows, my stomach, my neck, of course, but that's become a dumb cliché, jowls, upper thighs, fuck it, let's do it all," the woman in the green dress says.

Someone they knew had her full face cut around the edges, pulled back, and sewn up, and she looked like a different person, "in a good way."

"Yes, temporary mummification, let's call it. Re-humaning, the do-over menu. I'm down," white dress says.

"Look, there they go," green dress says, gesturing to the lawn where the TV newsman and the writer woman are walking, about twenty paces apart and in separate directions, toward the building. One goes in the downstairs back door, and the other walks around the side of the building where the auction has begun.

"Brazen," green dress says.

"Zero fucks, apparently, or maybe they think they are being more discreet than they are."

"We should go in," green dress says, and white dress turns toward the open double doors, but neither one of them actually goes. Instead, green dress takes a flask out of her small bag that's beaded to look like a bumble bee, and they pass the flask between them.

A low horn sounds out on the street on the other side of the stone wall, and both women startle and then start laughing.

"That sounded like a fucking ship," white dress says.

"A ship to take us somewhere. That's what I want. Should we go flag down the truck and have him transport us to the water?"

Instead, they step forward in their spiked shoes. Green dress puts the flask back in her bag. They're still laughing, too hard, probably. The music stops, and someone starts talking into a microphone.

White dress puts her finger to her lips. "Okay, let's go."

The daughter of the writer, sometimes at night, walks through the zoo in Woodley. It's easy to get out of her apartment, down the tiled stairs, out the brass-edged doors, and onto the street. Her mom is always in her little sister's room because what was once a need (her sister struggling to sleep, insisting on a grownup in the room) is now a habit (her mom wanting closeness, black-out blinds, white noise machine, and to be needed).

At night when she walks, almost everyone is locked in houses, apartments, on rectangular soft slabs, their bodies readying them for morning, but all the daughter wanted was to be out. She wants to see people sleeping in the park, to see bats making their strange patterns across the sky, to hear ambulances not so far away.

Once, she walked down a path that bypassed the zoo gate, past the cheetahs, the bison, the path to the pandas. She sat on a bench near the golden lion tamarinds, and there, on the next bench a few feet down, was a woman in a silk robe and fleece-lined slippers over otherwise bare feet. Her black hair was clipped at the back of her neck.

The whole zoo was cawing and calling, the animals, celebratory in the absence of humans, or so it seemed to the girl. The woman in the silk robe had a flask, and she offered it to the girl, and she drank from it.

"This is the best time," the woman said. "Empty, middle of the night. The nobody that's not there, or is it the nothing? I can't remember."

The girl wasn't sure what the woman was talking about, but she was happy to sit in silence, happy, too, when after how much time the girl couldn't tell, the woman stood, waved, and walked off, and the girl was left with the dark greenery around her closing in in the most pleasing way.

The girl wanted, heretofore or whatever other archaic word might make it official, for all her interactions to be like that, easy, with a minimal exchange of words and clear understanding of purpose, and just women.

Green dress and white dress stand toward the front, close to the stage.

The old nodding/smiling couple bids on the violinist. "She's really no trouble," the announcer says. "Look at how she holds the violin just so."

A woman with frizzy hair pushes through the crowd and elbows green dress as she goes. She spills and leaves a wide wet spot on the green fabric and a purple edible flower that sticks to her belly.

"Shit!" green dress says and dabs at her dress with a cocktail napkin. Green dress plucks the flower, slides it in her mouth, and shrugs. "It's not a party until you get spilled on, I guess," and white dress laughs.

"Oh my god, remember when we did this? Remember when this was us," white dress says and points her chin to the stage.

They're quiet for a minute, remembering, while people's paddles fly up.

Different girls trail off the stage on the arms of different people.

The girls are so many things but also a lot of the same thing. Lithe. Vessels. Giving but not needing. With few words. Troubled but undemandingly so. Slender. Big eyes, wide set in the face. Wanting but not needing. Sleek. Striking or stunning, either. Sexy but not overly so. Is servile the wrong word? Tempestuous but in the way of a single burst of wind that dies down quickly. Young.

"Well, cheers to being past all of that," green dress says to white dress.

White dress says, "Right of fucking passage. Here's to being women now." They clink glasses, though both, again, are empty.

The writer's daughter is up on the stage. The announcer is saying something about her intellect: "Just the right amount." The writer doesn't want to watch, so she walks over to the bank of windows. Ground lights are positioned at the bases of some of the trees, so the trunks are bright, and the branches are illuminated. The woman wants to pull her daughter off the stage and up one of the trees and cast walnuts or acorns or twigs at anyone who tries to come for her.

Instead, she leans her forehead on the glass and looks outside. The TV man is now standing near the stage with his wife, and the woman can see him reflected in the glass, his strong-jawed face, the face that makes so many people, not her, watch and feel calm and taken care of.

The woman scans the dark lawn for movement. Nothing. It's not until she looks right down at her feet, at the patch of limestone immediately on the other side of the glass door, that she sees it: the coyote. It is, she sees now, a coyote. "It's not like you're a fucking wildlife biologist, Mom," she can imagine her daughter saying. Still, she knows what she sees.

The woman hears the announcer saying something more about her daughter. She's too far from the stage now and can't make out the words, but she hears the crowd give a polite laugh.

The coyote is sitting the way a good dog would, waiting, its head cocked to the side, and she sees it's missing most of one ear, and its paw is mangled, so something has happened to it. The woman opens the door and lets it in.

The Last Summer

Several doctors had told him he was going to die, that it was a matter of months and not years. He was young for it, only fifty, and he'd fucked around most of his life, wandered, accomplished little, hadn't written a novel or gone to New Zealand or had a child. Also, the timing, during a pandemic, was not ideal, but then there was a sense of being pulled along by the tenor of the moment. This was to be a year of death, and he, Adam Zanger, was IN IT.

Each summer day, during what he assumes will be his last summer, he does his adjunct job, begging Kansas farm kids to think anything at all about poems. Each night, still alive and feeling basically the same, he sits in the garden of his rental house while whole families walk by on the brick sidewalk and peer over the stone wall at his flowers. There he is, like a zoo animal, amid the flash of hollyhocks and hibiscus, smoking weed, needlepointing lyrics from a Dead Kennedys song he hopes to turn into a pillow, a pillow for whom, down the road, he isn't sure.

On the first Friday evening in September, two women enter his garden through the back gate and take selfies up against a stand of rangy coreopsis. They don't see him in his metal chair behind a shield of potted succulents next to the house's side door.

"This is so aesthetic," one of them says. They both wear floral crop tops and high-waisted jean shorts that deny the existence of rib cages. The stone house where he lives is divided into two apartments, one up and one down. The upstairs unit has been empty all summer, after a grad student finished his PhD and moved back to Korea, so all through June, July, and August, Adam blasted music with windows open and thought about slamming his body into other bodies as he did forever ago at all the hardcore shows he attended in his teens and twenties, the raw thrill of blood in his mouth some nights, of spitting the shiny sea of it into gravel in the parking lot on his way to someone's car.

The women in his garden are jarring; first because the garden is his. He's grown it up from nothing over the last ten years. But next, because the only person he's been seeing regularly all summer, aside from random masked colleagues next to the mailboxes in the English department office, is his mom, Elaine, who, once a week, sits with him and drinks iced tea and rants about politics. She doesn't know the severity of his cancer. He downplayed it initially, and now some part of him is convinced he's being kept alive by how beholden he is to her unknowingness.

"Uh, hey, girlie," one of the women in his garden says to the other and then moves her eyes in Adam's direction and makes them big, which they are already because of the half-spiders of false eyelashes weighing down her eyelids.

"So, I think you're in our yard," the shorter one says. She stamps her foot in the grass like a pony. He hasn't seen them move into the upstairs unit, and he hasn't heard anything, but here they are.

During the years he's taught college English, the amount of variation between sorority people and non-sorority people in this Midwestern college town with a too-big Greek population has diminished enough that he doesn't always know which kind of person he is dealing with. At one point, he was able to tell, for example, when he shouted the lines of "Bantams in Pine-Woods," which of them flinched slightly and which nodded slightly, and then he knew which people to look more at when lecturing and which people to write off. But that has changed in the last few years, and now he could stand on a desk chair and read "The Bad Old Days" at high volume, almost shouting about the evil being clean and easy to find, and they would all stare into their laps at their glowing phones, and then how was he to know?

His last girlfriend left him a few years ago because she thought he was "too critical" and "so quick to judge," but he liked to call it "discerning." It was probably easier to be alone and think thoughts like "Oh, fuck, I have to live the last months of my life with sorority girls as my closest contacts" than to say them out loud and be called "maybe not a very nice person" by someone you shared a Tom's of Maine toothpaste with.

The cadence of this young woman's sentence, the woman who reaches out and plucks a bloom off a stem of bee balm, suggests immediately: sorority girl. This week, he's seen so many of them in swarms on campus in matching T-shirts and plastic leis and clunky white sneakers that look like they've been walking through and temporarily gotten stuck in vats of stucco, all of them shouting things from the old brick mansions where the younger ones live together in the way that cults do. She, shorter one, starts to walk toward him. Her hair is dark but with blond tips that tremble around her belly button. Her features are rounded: nose, chin, cheeks, all like a baby's.

For many months after his diagnosis, he was a zealot about distancing and masks. He went through a round of radiation and chemo that didn't work, and it mattered not at all that for months he triple-masked in the oncology waiting room. "Well, it didn't quite take," the doctor said, and Adam stopped going to appointments. For a few weeks, he mainly hid inside and ate Doritos and smoked. Eventually, he came out of it. He started eating good food again, started watching birds at the bird feeder, talked to people in the department office sometimes, grew things from seed under grow lights in the mudroom of his apartment, ordered custom needlepoint projects to have something to do with his hands that wasn't his phone. The first one was Plath, a line about dying being an art and doing it well, which is, for him, a lie. He isn't doing it well. He feels, more than anything, like a flight prolonged forever at a gate, a pointless stuffed metal tube over concrete.

He can play the situation with the women in his garden in two ways. He could apologize and disappear into his house and relinquish the garden to them, pretend it's a shared space and defer to them when they want to lug out a card table and invite over ten dudes named some version of "Brody" for beer pong. Or he could do this: "Actually, I live here. This is my garden. The upstairs apartment has the other side entrance and can make use of the side yard on the other side of the house, per the lease." Throwing in *per* is a low blow, but it is also how he's feeling.

"Really? I don't think so," the shorter one says, clearly the power player. "I am certain the landlord told us otherwise."

Otherwise.

"I don't think so." He doesn't move from his metal chair. They also don't move from where they stand, a foot from him, their shadows descending. He decides to cave. "That said, I've got some weed I'm happy to share."

They look at each other, short crop top to tall crop top. Tall crop top's hair is long too, but straight and thick. She seems like someone who rides horses.

"I'm Lane," the shorter one says. She doesn't extend any part of her body as greeting. Rather, she crosses her arms over her chest, and it buoys her tits.

He can't get excited by tits anymore, even young ones. Sure, he can imagine the way these tits might feel taut in his hands, but he doesn't care. He'd prefer a fizzy European soda and some malted milk balls from the place downtown that sells expensive things from other countries. He'd prefer to smoke in his yard with his limbs completely doused in OFF! and not think about things like bodies at all.

"I'm Carson," the other woman says.

He lights a joint and passes it. He doesn't worry about Covid now, and neither, apparently, do they. They each take a hit, and when it comes back to him, he has another. They talk about the following, and he mainly listens: covens, cottagecore, Taylor Swift's TikTok, dogs for your astrological sign, and how using feminized versions of words (actress, for example) is actually empowering. "Who doesn't want a whole category of word to just blossom into, to really own, nothing men can even claim? *Actress.* It's beautiful.

It's perfection." Lane sits in the grass cross-legged and closes her eyes. She does yoga-meditation hands. Carson follows suit.

Lane opens her eyes: "If my dad wasn't so on me to *have a career* and *make money*," Lane says, "I'd totally live in a cabin in the woods and knit all my clothes like whatshername the VP's daughter and bathe in a stream and do spells and potions at night."

"Same, totally," Carson says, and the sun drops completely out of sight.

It becomes a routine. Carson and Lane hang out with him in the garden before going off to presumably louder and bigger things. After dinner, he goes to the garden, and they clomp down the stairs in their heavy shoes. On the first night, they say, "Are you gay?" No, he is not. On the second night, they say, "Then where is your wife?" He does not have one. On the third night, they say, "Are you going to murder us?" No, it would take both energy and interest, and he has neither. On the fourth night, they say, "Do you know anything about astral projection?" No, he does not.

In fact, he's been thinking a lot about floating. Yoga people, leftists, freethinkers, wanderers, poets talk a lot about letting go, but he doesn't think those people have any fucking clue what that means, how, once you know you will have to let go, that you're almost there, you can't cling to anything. Nothing sticks, how it's some real fucking floating in the way of a piece of timber near a waterfall. Going, going, gone. As a kid, he lived in a house on a hill, and most of his summer days between second and third grade consisted of trying to build elaborate dams at the midpoint of the hill and then blasting the dams with hose water to see what they could withstand. It never took very much to loosen the sticks and branches and tall grasses and gathered stones and caked-on mud, and then, with it all in shambles on the gravel drive, he and his neighbor would start again.

On the fifth night, Lane says, "You know, Carson has a boat. It's not, like, a big deal, just a small motorboat. Sometimes when we hate the world, we go out there. It's her dad's, I mean, but he doesn't care. And the lake isn't that far."

The three of them end up in Carson's MINI Cooper, high and also sharing a White Claw, which is as blandly, beautifully terrible as he thought it would be. It's good/bad in the way of jellybeans, but liquid, and there's a thrill to it all. "I'm a sorority girl," he almost yells through the open sunroof as they pass the long shadows of light poles in parking lots, the brushy loom of trees encasing the same suburban house over and over.

The other day he Sharpied a line from "Plea for a Captive" on the wall above his bed, something about how you need to either kill everything or let it loose. He was no longer in a position to worry about things like security deposits. He could imagine one of his students seeing it and saying, "Oh, Jesus, get over yourself." Maybe that's what he needed to do: kill what he thought he wanted, what he thought he'd be, any and all ideas of the future. The dock, when they get there, is a string of wooden teeth over water.

In the boat, his legs are like those bendy toys of his childhood. The water slaps against the fiberglass, and some of it hits his face. He licks it off and he feels immediately stupid for thinking, *This tastes like sorrow.*

It's Carson's family's boat, but Lane stands at the wheel, turns over the motor, backs out too quickly. Her teeth flash white in the one yellow light that hangs from a rotting post near the dock. "Ooh, it's witchy out here, and I love it," Lane says, and then, "If you were going to kill us, this would be the time, though we could probably overpower you. Know that."

"Though maybe I once was, I am no longer interested in brutality," Adam says and leans his head back to look at the dark sky, where the moon, almost as if preordered, is bloated and obscured partially by one perfectly filmy cloud. If he closes his eyes like this, he can bring himself to the place of intersection, of being so much in his body that he feels no pain (as in the punk shows where all he wanted was more and more rigorous contact) or so out of it that he feels nothing at all (as in drifting, as in nonthinking, as in, maybe, death, but he doesn't know). How weird it is in life to go from maybe leaning into your own mother, scared in the night, hungry in the kitchen in the morning, tired and home from school, to leaning into some adult person not in your family or walking out into the night away from the home you've lived in for your entire childhood and not knowing at all what is to come. So much of life is about possibility, about what is next, what place what person what food, will this or that thing disappoint your family, will you travel, will you fuck someone, what are you going to buy, what time to sleep and wake up and what job and not job and what time this and that and that and then how suddenly, all of it simply, quite simply, doesn't matter. It's one of those things school didn't cover. It wasn't talked about or taught, as so many of the important things weren't. He wants to petition the university to teach classes in things like "become a person apart from your mother" or "living alone for a decade: making it work" or "dying: nobody wants to, but here we go."

"We need to get to the absolute middle of the lake," Lane says. "That's what we always do. Get out there, cut the lights, drift." She's still the one steering, and when she talks, she turns her head like an owl while keeping her body forward. It's the kind of boat with an awning over a spot where the captain stands at a wheel. The back has padded seats in a U, and when she guns the motor, droplets wrap around their faces.

He can see a bonfire on another shore in the distance. The people around it yell what he thinks are Rolling Stones lyrics, something about the sunshine and boredom, and then they cheer and laugh. Lane kills the boat motor.

"Have you heard of DMT?" Lane asks after a few minutes. They are in what seems to be the middle of the lake.

Maybe he's heard of DMT. He's not sure. "I don't think so. Remind me."

"It's like this thing, this chemical your body releases when you die," Lane says. She's pulled a cigarette from a glove box and is smoking the way he presumes she thinks people in movies do.

"Molecule, not chemical," Carson says. She's eating shark gummies from a plastic grocery-store bag she pulled from a seat back, and her feet in the heavy white shoes and short socks with hearts on them are hanging over the side of the boat.

"I have no idea if that's right, but okay, whatever, girl. Anyway," Lane says. She comes and sits next to Carson, and Carson shifts so she's close to Lane, and they drape a big sweatshirt across their laps. There are no animal noises, just water with its repetitive hitting against the sides of the boat. "So, not to be morbid, but imagine you're dying. You're lying on a bed or wherever you are when you're dying, and something happens in your brain that makes it in this, like, state of euphoria. You're gone, but in that last moment, your brain tricks you, some bit of brain magic, and then suddenly, it's like the best night, like you're driving in the summer, windows down, and you just hang your head out the side, and it's just whoosh and happy, like that, forever."

"That's most of it, I mean, that basically sums it up. But some people, scientists maybe, think that's where we got this idea of heaven, like people who die and come back from it describe this perfect feeling and place, and it's probably all DMT, like the body creates its own heaven, and to people it feels like forever," Carson says. It's the most sustained thing he's heard her say. Lane has been the talker.

What would that thing be for him? His summer-night thing, his heaven? Maybe that's life, figuring out that thing, whatever it might be, and then you are, postdeath, forever in it. He doesn't even know. Once, during his first year of teaching, he wrote out all the words to the poem "Young" on a giant roll of paper that he draped across the front wall of the classroom because it was, at that time, the poem that gave him that sad/beautiful/fuzzy/ life feeling and one he thought would do the same for first-year college students. He can't remember the poem now, but he remembers the feeling, the nostalgia of being a kid alone with both possibilities and fear in a bubble of summer streetlight-yellow nighttime.

Carson tosses the empty candy bag on the floor of the boat. Adam doesn't say anything, though he knows the wind, when they start again, will carry it over the water. Some sad turtle will end up with it over its head.

"We're taking a world religions class. It's a requirement," Carson says. "The teacher wears a leather necklace. You know the type. He's obsessed with DMT."

"You know, in high school, I used to go to this booth at an antique mall where the man who worked there sold weird jewelry and bookmarks and shit made out of animal bones. He was really nice, and we always talked about whatever, like, the weather, food, horses, driving in the country, anything. One morning, my dad was reading the paper, and there was the bone-jewelry dude's face on the front, and I was like 'Oh, my god, I know him,' and my brother was all arch and rude, like 'Oh, my god, he's a serial killer.' Turned out he had like twenty dead bodies buried in his yard, and probably half the bones he was selling were human or something."

"Don't you think people would have recognized human bones?" Carson asks.

"Oh, my god, I don't know, Carson. Maybe so, maybe not. The point is, I was friends with a serial killer. It's so crazy!"

Lane starts the boat up again before anyone can say anything. A wall of bugs sails through the boat's front light, a whole tight galaxy of movement.

Lane steers the boat to a dock on the other side of the lake from where they started. "This isn't our dock," Carson says, her voice loud enough to carry over the motor. "No shit," Lane says. "I need to pee, though."

"Oh, my god, so do I! We are so synched."

"I love you, girlie," Lane says to Carson, and it's a throwaway, something people like this say to everyone they know.

"I love you," Carson says back, and Adam believes it because Carson will probably always be someone who loves other people more.

Lane tries several times to reverse to get close enough to
the dock but keeps failing, so they ask him to toss in the
anchor, and the three of them leap into the water in shoes,
clothes, everything. He is so sick of his own shit that being
in water, being doused and muddled and soaking, is the best
possible thing. He goes under, and when he comes up, eyes
bleary, hair dripping water into water, Lane and Carson are
on the sand on the shore, squatting and peeing and laughing.
He lets them finish, gives them a minute, before swimming
in. His own mother spent years fretting over his inability
to swim well. He remembers her actually saying, "What if
you fall off a boat, what are you going to do? Drown?" And
he didn't. He can't swim well, but he can swim well enough
to make it to the sand, where he at first lies in the muck. It
isn't good beach sand like the kind in a movie about surfing.
It's slimy and has the occasional half-gnawed, fly-dotted fish
carcass. Still, even at fifty, even sick as a dog, or so his dead
grandmother would say, he is fine. He can pull his arms
through the water and get himself from point A to point B
and he can flop dramatically onto the sand and breathe in, so
air fills his lungs to that point of fullness that almost hurts.

Carson takes her phone out of her back pocket. It is in one
of those waterproof envelopes, and he can't remember her
putting it in there. His phone, now soaked, is a dead piece
of plastic and metal in his pocket.

His mom, the only person who texts him anymore, will
try him in the morning, and the message will hang in
some netherworld. Something like *I'll bring cucumber soup
to you tomorrow, cucumbers from my garden*, sitting there in
phone oblivion.

Carson turns the brightness up on her phone, so it
glows in the way of an oracle. She turns on music Adam

doesn't recognize. It's the opposite of what he usually likes. It's not screaming and thrashing. It's slow and rhythmic and electronic.

"Vibey," Lane says, and she stands up and starts dancing. She kicks her big, wet white shoes off. Carson does the same. They are both dancing and spinning, all arms, octopus, bending, turning. The only light around them is Carson's phone.

Adam gets back in the water and swims out as far as he can, until the two women are dots of movement on shore. He won't go under. He won't drown. He lies back and floats and lets words roll in at random: world and face and evening and long and women and river.

He treads water and wishes his mother could see him as he holds himself afloat, as he keeps going. What will he do? He's stopped himself short of thinking this in the past, but now he knows: he will move in with his mom when he needs to. He will die right there in his childhood bed, where he has before thrown up, shit himself, masturbated, dreamed of things, wondered, slept and slept and slept. Really, all of life is contained in a day anyway. Wake up its own little birth, and sleep a death, and all of whatever in between.

On the way back from the lake, they're wet on the leather seats. They stick, and the stickiness is beautiful and not bothersome. They're laughing on the speed bumps. The sound of the cicadas is delightful and not irksome. No cars pass them. They sing, and it fills the car with lovely noise. The lights are a beautiful blur alongside their speeding. If he closes his eyes, it is always nighttime and summer. He can never not think of this.

Acknowledgments

Thank you to everyone at Stillhouse Press and the amazing Rebecca Burke for the early encouragement, for her eagle eye, her real care for the project, and for helping me see how to shape these stories into a book. Stillhouse is a lovely collaborative effort engaging both writing and art students in the process, and I'm thrilled my book could be shepherded along by so many talented people.

I have such gratitude to the magazines and editors who first accepted and helped polish some of these stories: Evelyn Sommers at *The Missouri Review*; S. Tremaine Nelson and Nicky Gonzalez at *Northwest Review*; Courtney Harler, Marguerite Alley, and Suzanne Grove at *CRAFT*; Kait Heacock, Lisa Locascio, and Kate Folk at *Joyland Magazine*; Michael Griffith, Lisa Ampleman, and Toni Judnitch at *Cincinnati Review*; Jake Wolff at *Florida Review*; Emily Everett at *The Common*; Wendy Wimmer at *Witness*; Aram Mrjoian and Carrie Muehle at *TriQuarterly*; Jodee Stanley at *Ninth Letter*; Julie Schulte at *Faultline*; and Joanna Luloff at *Copper Nickel*.

People at small and independent presses and magazines are often there for the love of literature, for the ability to put work into the world unbeholden to larger industry pressures, and their commitment, often on a volunteer basis, is a beautiful thing.

I've been working alongside so many fiercely talented writers and editors at *Split Lip Magazine* for several years, and this community has been invigorating, inspiring, and sustaining. On this front, the uber-talented writers and editors Maureen Langloss and Janelle Bassett: you are the best writer friends (and friend friends) a person could hope for. Thanks, also, to Richard Mirabella and Mike Wilson for bringing your insight to many of these stories and to G.C. Waldrep, Tom Lorenz, and Mary Klayder for seeing something in my work many years ago.

Thank you to my friends Cat Hollyer, Tara Wenger, Hannah Hurst, and Allyson Tearnan for your kindness, creativity, and humor. You are such great humans.

I'm fortunate to have a close-knit, extended family, all of whom are supportive, inspiring, funny, and generally wonderful: Jack & Barb, Penny & George, Bonny, Helen, Laura, Eric & Lily, David, Catherine, Hailey & Leo, Jana, Jen, all the Pattersons, Moellers, Smiths and everyone else. A special shout-out to my sister, Laura, and my mom, Penny, for reading probably everything in here maybe more than once.

And, finally, to my little family: Matt, Edie, and Ben Patterson, all three spectacular writers themselves, all three the best walking, travel, and drive-around companions, the most interesting and caring people I know, always bringing insight, humor, and joy. All the thanks and all the love.

About the Author

Amy Stuber's writing has appeared in the *New England Review*, *Flash Fiction America*, *Ploughshares*, *The Idaho Review*, *Cincinnati Review*, *TriQuarterly*, *American Short Fiction*, *Joyland*, and elsewhere. She's the recipient of *The Missouri Review*'s 2023 William Peden Prize in fiction, winner of the 2021 *Northwest Review* Fiction Prize, and runner-up for the 2022 *CRAFT* Short Fiction Prize. Her work received a special mention in Pushcart Prize XLIV, appeared on the *Wigleaf* Top 50 in 2021, has been nominated for Best of the Net, and appears in Best Small Fictions 2020 and 2023. She has a PhD in English, has taught college writing, and worked in online education for many years.

You can find her work at www.amystuber.com.